"Dumb" Orphans

Orphans have been hidden victims of the HIV / AIDS epidemic in southern Africa. Cabrini Ministries staff working in the region observed the following: 'After 20 years of sickness and dying and then 10 years of recovery with antiretroviral drugs (ARVs), families have disintegrated. Orphans, many thousands of them, are struggling to raise themselves with no sense of belonging to a family, a group, a Nation. They are learning that adults often take advantage of them, encroach on their homesteads, abuse them physically and sexually, or just don't have time for them because the adults themselves are overburdened with mouths to feed.' (www.cabriniministries.org / category / articles /).

This story is a tribute to the indomitable spirit of children who have lived through such experiences and survived and even prospered.

What readers have said about "Dumb" Orphans

A very touching and inspiring storyline, enhanced with some beautifully evocative descriptions and imagery, which ends on a positive and uplifting note. It also provides fascinating information on aspects of African culture, geography and the environment.

The Writers' Advice Centre for Children's Books

The Bundu Bunch Trilogy is an overall positive tale of family support, teamwork and working hard to overcome obstacles. Through the plotline of the different stories there's a gentle introduction to discussion of poverty, international aid, immigration and refugees and more. With illustrations depicting key scenes at the end of some chapters this represents an easy way to introduce these topics for younger readers.

LoveReading4Kids Ambassador

"Dumb" Orphans

The Bundu Bunch Trilogy

ALLAN LOW

Illustrated by Elizabeth Sparg

© Allan Low, 2022

Published by Bundu Bunch Publishing

A CIP catalogue record for this book is available from the British Library.

ISBN 978-1-7390813-0-0

Book layout by Clare Brayshaw

Cover and book illustrations © Elizabeth Sparg

Prepared and printed by:

York Publishing Services Ltd
64 Hallfield Road
Layerthorpe
York YO31 7ZQ

Tel: 01904 431213

Website: www.yps-publishing.co.uk

To the memory of Anne, Mum, Gogo

By buying this book you have made a donation to
The SHAMBA Trust of the full price paid if
purchased from www.ypdbooks.com.
Net of retailer charges otherwise.
Thank you.

…...children collecting brushwood, tending herds, cutting grass for the cattle……but the child's biggest role is in the home: he is responsible for supplying water. While everyone else is still asleep, little boys are rising in the darkness and running to springs, ponds, rivers – for water.

More about the children … Hunger for these children is something permanent, a way of life, second nature. And yet they do not ask for bread or fruit, or even for money.

They ask for a pencil.

They would all like to go to school, they would like to learn.

Ryszard Kapuściński,
The Shadow of the Sun: My African Life

Contents

BOOK I

Aiyasha's
Bottomless Briefcase

Contents

Chapter 1

My orphan family

I sat on the upper slopes of our valley and watched the children pour out of the community school below me.

'What have they learnt in their classes today that I have missed?' I wondered wistfully. 'There was a time when I could have been in those classes, and my future could have been equally as bright as theirs.'

Then the sun came out from behind the clouds and washed away the shadows that had been on the land and in my mind. I looked up at the grassy slopes above me and the rocky mountain above them. I looked at the crop fields and the glinting river below me and my heavy mood began to lighten.

I shook my head and said to myself, 'There is so much to explore and discover in this valley with my fellow orphans. Maybe I can learn enough to do well, even without any classes.'

Then I heard the booming voice of the headman of our community telling the children not to linger, but to hurry back to their homes to help their mothers gather water and firewood and cook the food, and my head hung heavy again.

* * *

I am Sipho. I'm an orphan, but I think of myself as a lucky orphan as I have a family of my own. I am seven years old. I live with my sister Jabu and our five cousins, who are also orphans. We look after ourselves. Well, almost. Aiyasha, who is fifteen, is in charge. We mostly do what she tells us to.

I like living with my sister and cousins. We are all about the same age. My sister Jabu is six. Our eldest cousin is Monica. She is seven, like me. Then there are the two boy twins, Langa and Jacob, who are five. Sakhile is also six and her brother Luke is five.

We don't have much. No Lego, no puzzles, no board games, no toys, no books, no football. But we have ourselves and our surroundings. We love to explore together and discover things about the valley in which we live. The valley is called Bundami and is in the southern part of Africa. The river, the rocks, the animals and plants in the Bundami valley constantly give us new things to wonder at, to test and to admire. Because we spend so much time exploring the wild, we call ourselves the Bundu Bunch.

There is also a toddler in the household. She is not a member of the Bundu Bunch because she is too young to join our explorations. She is just two years old and we call her Elah. This is short for Elahlekile, which means lost. My sister Jabu found Elah down by the river a year ago when we went to fetch water.

'Hey, Sipho,' called Jabu. 'There is a small child here in the long grass. She is wrapped in a blanket and seems to be asleep.' We looked for the owner of the child and called out. But there was nobody around.

'Poor little thing,' I said, 'not being wanted by anyone in her family.'

'Poor family,' responded Jabu, 'to feel they have no alternative but to abandon their child.'

Then Jabu said, 'I am going to take this little child to the community leader. You must finish filling the water containers and take them back up the hill by yourself.'

This was typical of my bossy sister Jabu. She liked to be the playmaker, deciding on what action we should take and who was to do what and how.

My sister has fixed ideas about how things should be and gets upset when others don't agree with her. But what I like about my sister is that she never stays upset for long and is soon laying down the law again on another matter.

I didn't argue with Jabu on this occasion. Using the blanket to secure the now-stirring child onto her back, she gave me one of her knowing smiles and set off towards the leader's compound.

One of the water containers was already full and it didn't take me long to fill the other one. Getting the two ten-litre containers back up the hill on my own was another matter. You should try carrying ten litres of water uphill. I had to take one container up the slope a few yards, put it down and then come back for the other one.

I made good progress on the flat valley bottom but, when I got to the steeper slopes of the valley sides, I had to go through maize fields. There was a path, but it was narrow and the maize was much taller than me and there was no breeze in the maize tunnels. There were ten terraces of maize fields before our hut. I was getting hotter and slower. By the time I reached the end of the third terrace, I started to wish I had argued about this plan with my sister. It was unfair to expect me to do this alone. I thought of emptying half the water to lighten the load, but I couldn't bring myself to do that. To us, every drop of water is precious and I didn't want to face what the others would say and think if I came back with half-full containers.

Jacob I didn't worry about. He was happy-go-lucky and wouldn't say anything. Jacob's twin brother, Langa, and Luke would whine for a bit, but soon focus back on their latest project. The girls would be less forgiving. Monica would worry that the maize porridge would not be properly cooked. Jabu would criticise me for not making an alternative plan, and Sakhile would ask how much I proposed allocating between washing versus cooking versus drinking.

Aiyasha, I knew, would sort it all out and be sympathetic. But I thought it best to avoid the flack.

* * *

When I got to our hut, I was exhausted and sat in the open shelter beside it. This, like the hut, had a tin roof which gave shelter from the sun; but, unlike the hut itself, it did not heat up like an oven from the moment the sun rose above the mountain. We called this the stoep. This is where the cooking pot was kept, where we ate our meals, met together and talked and laughed together.

Jabu had been back a little while. She poured water from one of the containers into the cooking pot, which she then put on the fire that Jacob had lit with the wood he had brought down from the forest.

I saw the dust cloud first. Then came the sound of the old engine and then the gruff voice of our leader as he got out of the truck.

'Urgh, you, Aiyasha. You will take care of this baby. The father has left the community and the mother has been taken to the clinic. You will keep it here in the orphan hut.'

I looked at Jabu. She looked surprised and angry.

She whispered to Aiyasha. 'We can't manage the child here. That is why I took her to the headman's house, so he could find someone in the community who would be willing to take care of her.'

'It's OK, Jabu,' said Aiyasha. 'We will look after her.'

Aiyasha knew it was no use trying to confront our community headman. We had to do what he decided, always.

The headman lifted the whimpering child roughly out of the back of the truck and thrust her into Aiyasha's arms.

'Keep this until its mother comes back,' he instructed, then he returned to his truck and drove off.

Elah's mother never did come back, so Elah became the youngest member of our orphan family.

Chapter 2

Our headman: Meyego

Each community has a headman who is appointed to be the community leader. Our headman is Mr Meyego. We don't say Mister in our country. Instead, we say Nkosi as a polite way of addressing a senior man.

We all look to Nkosi Meyego to tell us what to do. Everyone in the community says we have him to thank for whatever we have. Which, as I've said, as far as we are concerned is not much.

Meyego has a briefcase. According to Meyego, his briefcase contains 'the Bundami community'. Not literally, of course, because the whole community cannot fit in there. By 'community' Meyego means the preferences and desires of everyone living in the Bundami valley. Meyego regards his briefcase as the symbol of his authority over the people of Bundami, and he takes it everywhere with him. After all, the briefcase is a very smart briefcase and nobody in the community has a briefcase as grand as his.

Meyego is a big man. He has a big, booming voice, a big smile, a big belly and a big ego. Sometimes, he plays nice to us orphans. He sometimes drives past our hut in his big pickup truck and gives us something out of it.

The other day, Meyego came round the corner tooting his horn loudly.

'Where are my orphans?' he called out as he eased his bulk down from his truck, smiling broadly. 'I have something special for you today.'

The back of his truck was full of food. There were big bags of maize and rice, and sacks of chickpeas, sugarbeans and soup powder. There were also vegetables: sweet potatoes, cabbage, spinach, beans and carrots. And lots of fruit: sacks of oranges, mangoes, avocados, bananas and pineapples. We also saw loaves of bread, and buns and cakes.

For us, feeling hungry is normal. But when we see food like this, our hunger becomes painful. We yearn for our stomachs to feel full and we yearn for our mouths to be treated to tasty bites. Our eyes focused on the buns and cakes. But we also hoped for some of the rice and maize to fill our bellies.

Meyego put a bag of maize and a bag of sugarbeans on the ground.

'Urgh, Aiyasha,' he commanded. 'Make sure you make this last for the next four weeks, until you get your next government orphan feeding programme rations.'

'Thank you, Nkosi Meyego,' said Aiyasha, politely. 'The children would really love to taste a bun. Would you spare one for each of us, please?'

Meyego's smile disappeared. 'I give this food to the families in the community who deserve it,' he said with a low growl. 'Not to dumb orphans who are only a burden on our community.'

'But, Nkosi Meyego, we fetch your water and firewood and look after your cattle in the fields,' responded Aiyasha.

Meyego had already squeezed his bulky belly behind the steering wheel of his truck and had started the engine. He left in a cloud of dust, without a smile on his face.

Meyego is not interested in us doing anything to better ourselves. He says 'Orphans are dumb and are a burden on the community.'

Meyego thinks of us as a burden on the community because we cannot pay him for things he provides, like the food he brings from the town. And he calls us dumb because we have not been allowed to go to school and don't know much about letters and numbers.

Chapter 3

Before the illness and long ago

I haven't always lived in the orphan hut with my, now, family. You see, there was an illness. Before the illness, my sister and I were living with our five cousins in a large compound in the middle of the Bundami valley. In the compound there were eight thatched houses called rondavels, because they were circular. The biggest rondavel was for the head of the compound. The others were for his wives and their children. It was wonderful to have so many children to play with. We were looked after by Aunt Beatrice. Aunt Beatrice was like a mother to us all, although she was not the real mother of any of us.

My mother and her two sisters used to send money to Aunt Beatrice at the end of each month. This was the money they were earning in the textile factory in the capital city. Each year, our mothers took two weeks' leave from the factory to come and help with the maize harvest. Last harvest time, our mothers spoke to us before they returned to the factory.

My mother said to me and my sister, 'I love you both very much and I wish I could be with you here more of the time. But you know I need to go to the factory to earn money to support you. The good news is that the factory owner has told your aunts and me that we will be promoted to be supervisors next year. That means we will be earning more money. With the extra money, we will be able to buy school uniforms for you and pay school fees. Next year, you will go to the school in the valley to start your education.'

I felt elated. This is what I had hoped for. My mother had told me and my sister, many times before, how important it was to have an education, to be able to pass exams in order to get good jobs and to prosper. That night, I thought to myself how wonderful it was that we were going to get the education that would give us the opportunity of a bright future.

But I also had a less happy thought. 'We would have to help Aunt Beatrice with the chores, like fetching water and firewood, when we came back from school. That would mean less time for exploring the bush together as the Bundu Bunch.'

As I fell asleep, I persuaded myself that we could do both.

* * *

Back then, we helped with the chores in the morning and had the afternoon to ourselves, to do whatever we liked. When the weather was hot, we went to the waterfall at the top of the valley and swam in the pool below it. Monica and Jacob would not sit on the warm rocks for long to dry out. They soon went off hunting.

Monica would say, 'I'm just going to find some of those mushrooms that you all said helped to make the maize porridge taste so good last week. I'll be on the other bank. Call me when you are heading back.'

Jacob would go off without saying anything. Jacob hunted for insects and animals, both in the water and on the banks of the river. Sometimes, he didn't get back to the compound until well after dark.

The rest of us alternated between swimming in the cool water, ducking under the cascading shower at the bottom of the falls and returning to the rocks to dry off and warm up.

Our mothers taught Monica and me to swim when they were back from the factory one Christmas time, four years ago. I love it more than anything. In the water, I feel free and safe. I enter another place and imagine a world of my own. As I dive through the bubbles under the waterfall, I forget about my mother being far away, my missing father, and my doubts about whether I will ever be able to earn enough money so my mother can come home and live with my sister and me.

* * *

When it was not so hot, we went up the hill through the forest and climbed among the rocks. We talked about seeing our mothers again at Christmas when the factory closed for the holiday and they came back, usually with presents for us, Aunt Beatrice and Uncle Boniface.

Uncle Boniface was quite old and spent the day sitting under the large tree in the middle of the compound with a rug around his shoulders and holding his knobkerry walking stick. For most of the time, Uncle Boniface seemed to be asleep under the big tree. But at night, when we were gathered round the fire, his eyes became bright and his old arms became alive as he told us stories of the 'long-ago, on-the-go' people who used to live in this valley. When we were up on the mountain, we often talked about the stories that Uncle Boniface told us about the people who lived here a long time ago.

In that long-ago time, Uncle Boniface told us, there were no fields in the valley, just bushes and trees. Nobody lived in the valley because it was full of wild animals and it was too dangerous to sleep there. Lions might eat you. Elephants might trample you. Kudu bulls might skewer you. Buffalo might charge you. Oryx might spear you. Hyaenas might chew you. Wild dogs might tear you apart. Baboons might steal the babies. Scorpions might poison you. So everyone slept up on the mountain.

But the bushes and trees in the valley were full of berries and fruit, so the people would go down to the valley in the morning to get the food they needed for the day. They had to be very careful and watchful because behind the next bush there might be a dangerous animal, and on the branch of the next tree there might be a snake waiting to strike. Because of the danger around them, they never sat down to eat their food. They ate their breakfast, lunch and supper as they walked and watched out carefully for danger signs.

It was the same when they got to the river at the bottom of the valley. Unlike today, in that long-ago time the river was full of danger. There were hungry hippos, crafty crocodiles, terrible toads and cruel catfish, all looking for the opportunity to grab an unsuspecting person or child or baby. So these people learnt how to do everything on-the-go. Through the day, they did their drinking, washing, cleaning, peeing and pooing on-the-go.

Uncle Boniface told us lots of tales of the adventures these people had while they were gathering their on-the-go meals and living their on-the-go lifestyle. In some of the stories, everyone got back safely to the mountain at the end of the day. But, in some of the stories, a few did not.

Of course being on-the-go all day was very tiring. When they got back up the mountain, the people were all exhausted and they gathered together to sleep under the protection of a large, hanging rock. But they were still not completely safe. There was one danger that lived among the rocks. A leopard who hunted at night. Uncle Boniface told stories of how the people tried to protect themselves against the leopard. They built fences of sticks around themselves, but the leopard clawed through these to steal one of the sleeping group. They built walls of rocks around themselves, but the leopard managed to climb over these. They put one of their number on guard through the night, but often this person was so tired from being on-the-go all day that he or she had a problem staying awake and, as a result, couldn't be found in the morning.

Uncle Boniface told how eventually the on-the-go people learnt how to make fire. They noticed that grass fires started when there was a lightning storm. They came to realise that it was the heat of the lightning that started wild fires when the grass was very dry. They found they could make heat by rubbing sticks together. So they did this with dry grass piled around the sticks. The grass glowed red and then burst into flame. The leopard was frightened of fire and so the on-the-go people stayed safe at night.

Uncle Boniface also told us about the ruler of the on-the-go people. He was more advanced than the others as he did not lead an on-the-go lifestyle. He lived in a large, deep cave. The people brought him a basket of fruit and berries each evening and left it for him at a distance from the cave opening. Nobody went into the cave as it was protected by a family of cobras who lived in a hollow at the entrance, which was kept warm by the sun shining on the rocks around it all day. The ruler had a bamboo pipe which made a haunting noise when he blew into it. The cobras would be entranced by that sound and they let the ruler pass in and out unharmed.

Because the ruler was not on-the-go all day, he had time to think and the people came to him for advice on how to deal with their problems. He was a wise ruler and gave the on-the-go people good advice, like learning from lightning about how to make fire.

Uncle Boniface always ended his stories by telling us how we were very lucky that our great-grandparents and grandparents had developed modern ways of living so that we could be relieved of having to live the old on-the-go lifestyle. He said that this meant we had time to think and learn and to make our own decisions on how to handle problems. He told us that, if we saw people living on-the-go lifestyles, we were not to copy them, as that would be going backwards.

* * *

I enjoyed the carefree life we lived then. Even though I did not see much of my mother, I felt I had a bright future, especially as we were going to start school in the New Year. Then things changed and I never saw my mother again, and my future no longer seemed so bright.

Chapter 4

The illness

The illness changed everything.

The first we heard about it was when Aunt Beatrice called the seven of us together outside her rondavel and told us to sit down. She said that our mothers would not be coming back this Christmas. There had been an infection at the factory which had taken many lives, including those of our mothers.

The funeral began two days later. The community held a vigil which lasted for three nights. During this time, people came to our houses with gifts of food. There was much wailing and sorrow, as well as songs of thanks for the lives of the dead. On the third morning, there was a burial ceremony followed by a funeral feast.

Aunt Beatrice told us we must be strong and do as we were told by the headman. She said our mothers had been good people and had taken care of our needs, but from now on we would have to learn to manage our lives without the support our mothers had been giving us.

Of course, we were all very sad. Sad that we would not be able to see our mothers again, sad not to be getting any presents that Christmas, and sad because we would not be able to start school after all. We were also sad for Aunt Beatrice and Uncle Boniface. Without the support from our mothers, they would struggle to buy enough to feed and clothe us all.

Worst of all, my hopes for a bright future were shattered. How would I now get on in the world and do as well as others without going to classes?

That night, I snuggled up close to my sister and we held each other tight and cried ourselves to sleep. I expect our cousins in the other rondavels were doing the same.

After the funeral, Aunt Beatrice went to see headman Meyego to ask for his help in deciding what to do about caring for us orphans. She asked Meyego to call a community meeting so that people could discuss the issue and decide who would be able to help us, and how.

But Meyego would not call the community meeting.

'No need for that,' he said to Aunt Beatrice. 'I know what is best for the community. The community is in my briefcase. I will let you know what we plan for the orphans.'

And the 'community' decision that came out of Meyego's briefcase was the following.

We orphans were to go to the old hut at the far end of the valley and be looked after there by another orphan, Aiyasha. This would enable Meyego to apply to the government to register us as vulnerable orphans and he would then be able to claim government food aid. In this way, we would not be so much of a burden on the community.

As we said goodbye to Aunt Beatrice and Uncle Boniface, we saw sadness in their eyes, but also relief on their faces. I think Aunt Beatrice knew she would not be able to support us without the money from our mothers. The little she and Boniface received from their pensions was barely enough for the two of them.

We collected our few belongings, like our blankets, some spare clothes and Jacob's collection of butterflies, and started on the long walk to the hut at the far end of the valley. Standing in the doorway was Aiyasha. We had not seen her before. What we saw appalled us and impressed us. She was fifteen years old, but was not much taller than Monica, our eldest. Her face and body were scarred by old hunger sores and her arms and legs were like sticks. But her eyes were big and black and bright. With her eyes she was telling us that, no matter what she looked like physically, she was proud and serious and determined.

Aiyasha welcomed us with a warm smile.

'Hello, everyone. My name is Aiyasha and together we are going to make a strong family. I know you are sad to have lost your mothers and to leave your homes. I also have lost my parents and I have been sent here because my father was from Bundami. This is a new home for us all and we are going to make it a happy home, a caring home and a nurturing home. To do that, we all have to help each other and support each other. Can we do that?'

Of course, all seven heads in front of her nodded enthusiastically. We were used to supporting each other – after all, we didn't call ourselves the Bundu Bunch for nothing.

I thought, 'With a manager like Aiyasha, we can be an even stronger team.'

Then Aiyasha said, 'Let's get started by putting our things away in the hut.'

Aiyasha had already put her things in one corner. Like us, she hadn't come with much. She had a roll-up sleeping mat, a blanket and a cooking pot. And a briefcase. The briefcase was very old. It was big, baggy and battered.

* * *

We had been moved to the margins of the community and sent to live in an old hut at the far end of the valley.

Was I cross? Yes.

Was I downcast? Yes, but not quite as downcast as before.

After all, Aiyasha was just like one of us and seemed really strong. And the Bundu Bunch was together.

With those positive thoughts, I lay down on my mat to sleep and pulled my blanket over me. I looked around the new surroundings of our orphan hut and my eyes rested on the outline of the old, battered briefcase that stood up in the corner. I couldn't help contrasting it with the new, smart briefcase that belonged to Meyego. Two very different briefcases belonging to two very different people. The two people who now would have a strong influence on my new life and my prospects for the future. One of them, Aiyasha, the head of our new family, I felt positive about. But the other, the head of our community, filled me with feelings of foreboding. Which influence would prevail I wondered, with some concern?

My dream that night was of the two briefcases taking it in turns to come to the front and pushing the other one into the background. The way it ended I cannot remember.

Chapter 5

Pele joins the Bundu Bunch

Two weeks after we moved to the orphan hut, Monica went to visit Aunt Beatrice and Uncle Boniface. She came back with sad news. Uncle Boniface had died and Meyego had sent Aunt Beatrice back to her own family in a neighbouring community, which meant that we never saw her again. What was worse, was that Monica found out that Meyego had given the compound to his sister, Cebsile, and her family. None of us ever wanted to visit our old home again.

The day after Monica's visit to our old home, Meyego came by and told us that each day two of us must take his cattle to the grazing areas on the mountain. Jacob volunteered to be in this herding group because, while the cattle were grazing, he got the opportunity to do what he liked best: to hunt for animals and find out where they lived and what they got up to.

Jacob went high up the mountain one morning, while keeping an eye on the cattle below him. He followed a butterfly as it darted from bush to bush.

The butterfly alighted on a leaf of a bush and then was gone. It was there one moment and not the next. Jacob figured a frog or lizard must have eaten the butterfly, so he inspected the bush more carefully. What he saw was not a frog or a lizard, but a pair of big black eyes on a furry face.

Jacob thought he was looking at a rock rabbit, and wondered why it had not scurried away across the rocks as they usually did whenever he got near to one. The eyes continued to stare at him. Jacob gently pulled away the branches and saw why the animal had not run away. One of its back legs was stuck in a crack in the rock from which the bush was growing.

Jacob spoke softly to the animal as he felt the leg and tried to get it out of the rock crack. The leg was wedged in very tightly and it took Jacob a long time to gently turn it round and slide it out of the crack. When he had done this, Jacob saw that the leg was broken. That is when Jacob decided to bring the animal home to mend its broken leg.

Now that he had the animal in his hands, Jacob realised that it was a young mongoose. Jacob had watched a mongoose once doing battle with a snake, and had marvelled at how good and fast the mongoose was at striking at the snake's head and darting away. This gave him the idea of a name for his mongoose. Back when we were in our mothers' compound, Jacob had listened to older children and men talking about football. Very often, the talk included mention of the greatest striker in the world. He named his young mongoose after that striker.

It was late afternoon when Jacob got back to the hut with his newly named friend: Pele. I returned from delivering water to Meyego's compound and wondered what everyone was looking at so intently. Pele was on the ground, looking up at the admiring faces of the Bundu Bunch with his large, dark eyes.

For the next few days, Pele couldn't move around much and so was not able to catch his own food. We did that for him by catching frogs, crickets and caterpillars down by the river. We also served up worms, slugs, millipedes, cockroaches and spiders as well as pawpaw, avocado, mango and granadilla. Pele ate most things we gave him because he was very hungry. But he did draw the line at dung beetles. He would not eat dung beetles, however hungry he was.

Soon, his leg mended and Pele found his own food. Aiyasha said we could keep him as a pet because, unlike a dog, we didn't need to use any of our scarce food for him. Plus, he was catching and eating rats and snakes, which kept them away from the hut.

Pele always came with us on our discovery adventures, so he became the eighth member of the Bundu Bunch – and a very valuable member, as it turned out.

Chapter 6

Classless equals clueless

We orphans don't get to sit in any of the classes in the Bundami community school. Wonderful, you might think. How wonderful not to have to go and sit in school classrooms all day. No rushing to get ready for school, no standing still for ages at boring assembly. No hard benches and harder lessons. No horrible cold school lunches. No teachers ordering you about and giving you difficult things to do.

But you might actually decide these things are not too bad when you hear what we have to do instead. We have to be at Meyego's house before his son, Samu, leaves for school. Some of us have to collect the water containers for Meyego's family, while others have to go to the kraal and rouse his sleeping cattle. Some of us spend the day on the long walk to the river, where we fill the containers and then slowly haul their heavy loads back up the hill. The others have to find fresh grazing up on the hillsides for the cattle and make sure they don't wander too far and get lost. While the herders are on the hillside, they have to collect firewood for Meyego's wife to make the fire on which to cook his food. We don't get anything to eat all day. Your school lunches would seem like a rare feast to us.

So, the first reason that we don't go to the school is that Meyego's household requires us to do these chores so that Samu does not have to do them and can spend the day in the classroom. The second reason is that Aiyasha is unable to pay the school fees. The school fees go to the teacher, who is Meyego's sister, Cebsile. If families do not pay Cebsile at the start of each month, then their children are excluded from school. As I told you, Cebsile has taken over the compound where we used to stay with Aunt Beatrice and Uncle Boniface. She has built herself a new brick house there, with a proper stove for cooking, and everyone in her household has their own bed. You might think this is quite normal, but it represents a high level of luxury for my community in Bundami.

Of course, because we don't attend school classes, we don't know all the letters. We can't spell or write our names and we do not know how to do sums. Samu and his friends like to jeer at us orphans. They ask us questions that we cannot answer. They ask us our names and they challenge us to spell them out and write them in the sand. They ask us to count the mangoes on the big tree in the middle of Samu's compound. They tell us if we get the correct answer, we can have one each, but only if we then tell them how many mangoes would be left. And we also have to tell them how many each of us would get if we took all the mangoes on the tree and shared them amongst ourselves equally. We make some guesses, but we are always told the guess is wrong.

'Orphans know nothing, orphans know nothing,' they chant. They have made up a silly song about us:

Orphans are dumb.
They don't know their letters
And can't spell their name.
Oh dear, what a shame.

As for numbers:
They are a mystery for them.
Getting the answers
Is a guessing game.
Oh dear, what a shame.

They look like scarecrows,
All skin and bone.
They've lost their mums
And don't accept the blame.
Oh dear, what a shame.

We do not like being told we are dumb. So we asked Aiyasha how we could learn to write and do sums. Aiyasha said she would see what she could do.

'But,' she said, 'the problem is that the work you do for Meyego and his household takes you most of the day. By the time you finish collecting the water and return from taking his cattle to the grazing lands and finding firewood, you are all much too tired to do lessons. Also, there is not enough time before it gets dark, and you know we need to light the fire and cook our meal before the sun goes down.'

So, we had to accept the jeering from Samu and his friends. This made us angry and was one of the reasons we planned the bun raid.

Chapter 7

The bun raid

Every couple of weeks, the city bakery gives unsold buns to communities for their orphans and vulnerable children. However, none of these buns ever find their way to us. Meyego sells them to those who can pay. The last time Meyego came past our hut with the buns in the back of his truck, Aiyasha asked if we could each have one. He had driven off without responding and we had to endure the sight of these delicacies getting further and further away, with the only benefit to us being the imagination of their taste.

After supper one evening, we gathered around the cooking pot fire to discuss how we could do more than just imagine the taste of the buns.

Luke said we should just take some of the buns for ourselves when nobody was watching.

'But Meyego will notice that the buns are missing and he is sure to suspect us,' said Monica.

'Then we need to make sure he cannot pin it on us,' said Langa.

'How do we do that?' I said.

'We make it look like it was someone else,' said Jacob.

'Who?' said Jabu.

'Samu!' Langa, Luke, Jacob, Monica and I shouted all at once.

Now, we were getting quite excited about the idea of taking some buns for ourselves, especially if we could frame Samu at the same time.

Sakhile was the only one without a smile on her face. In a serious voice, she said, 'But that would be stealing and we shouldn't steal.' There was silence for a while and then Monica spoke up.

'We know the bakery wants the buns to be given to orphans and vulnerable children like us,' she said. 'So, I don't think it would be stealing if we take what is intended for us.'

We debated this thought for a while and decided that it would not be 'pure' stealing. I think it was Langa who came up with an acceptable way of thinking about it. He called it 'justified stealing'. We were all happy with this, though I think Sakhile was least happy.

Jabu led the discussion on the justified stealing plan. We agreed a course of action and decided to implement it that very night to take advantage of the clouds and lack of moon.

Jabu and the twins were selected for the raiding party. As we watched them leave for Meyego's compound and saw their dark outlines blend into the blackness, my stomach felt uncomfortably tight.

I went over the plan in my mind many times as we waited for the return of the raiding party. I'm sure the other three did as well.

Jabu was to go to the hut were Samu slept and find the new boots he was so proud of among the shoes everyone left outside the entrance. She was to put these on and walk to Meyego's truck, which was parked, with the buns in the back, near to the cattle kraal.

Meanwhile, the twins were to go to the kraal, which they knew so well as they went there every day. Langa and Jacob knew of some planks leaning against one side of the cattle kraal. They would place these in front of themselves and walk on them from the kraal to the truck, so as not to leave any footprints. They had two sacks with them and they would fill them with buns from the back of the truck.

Jabu would walk around the truck in Samu's boots and make sure they made strong footprints and became dusty with the red soil in that area. She would then walk back to Samu's hut and leave the boots where she found them.

That was the plan. But would Jabu, Langa and Jacob be able to implement it on this very dark night? Would they avoid being found out? I was imagining the things that could have gone wrong and what might happen to us if we were discovered.

After about half an hour, I couldn't help turning to Luke and whispering, 'Why aren't they back yet? Do you think they are OK?'

Luke just shrugged his shoulders. Like me, he was anxiously peering into the solid dark wall in front of us.

Then Luke sat up. 'Look!' He pointed to the silent shapes slowly separating the blackness. They were back!

'Hey, how did it go?' I asked excitedly. Jacob held up a sack with one hand and gave a thumbs-up with the other.

'It went like clockwork,' said Jabu.

We gathered round to listen to their accounts and savoured a bun each while doing so.

Now, we just had to wait and see whether our second objective of framing Samu would work as well.

Chapter 8

Samu's revenge

The day after the bun raid, our chores seemed to take much more effort than normal. The excitement, anxiety and late night had left us feeling tired. And we were still worried about the outcome once Meyego found out that the buns were missing.

That evening, supper was late. Jacob and Langa only got the fire going with the firewood from the forest as the sun was setting. Jabu and I had only managed to fill half of our water containers, so the maize was not so well soaked as usual and the porridge took longer to cook.

As we finished eating, Aiyasha spoke to us all.

'You all need an early bed tonight after last night's escapade.' With a half smile she added, 'The less I know about the details of what you got up to, the better. Then, if Meyego questions me, I can deny any knowledge.'

Her smile widened. 'But I would rather like to taste one of the buns, if there are any left.'

We all burst out laughing. Of course Aiyasha knew what we were up to, even though we thought she was sleeping through it all. There were two buns left for each of us, including Aiyasha.

As we ate them, we commented on the fact that we had not seen Samu that day.

* * *

The following day, again there was no sign of Samu. We learnt from his friends that Meyego had locked him in his room as punishment for stealing the buns. So that objective had worked as well!

That night after supper Monica said, 'I think we should give Jabu a big clap for leading such a successful "bun raid" plan.'

Jabu smiled broadly. But after the clapping died down, she put on her more serious face. 'Yes, it was a success,' she said. 'But I think it was much more than that. Think about what we did. We made Meyego punish Samu for us. That's truly amazing. We were able to get Meyego to do something for our benefit, without him realizing it. If we can do that, we can do anything.'

'We can do anything.' I went to sleep that night with Jabu's words playing over and over in my mind. As I drifted off to sleep the words became: *CAN DO, CAN DO, CAN do, can do, can....*

* * *

The whole of the week was bliss. Samu stopped jeering at us and his friends stopped singing their orphan song. Instead, Samu glowered at us. He knew that, dumb as we were, we had played a trick on him and got our own back.

We agreed it was good to have a let up from the jeering. However, Sakhile had her misgivings.

'It is nice to have got our own back on Samu,' she said, 'but I expect he will be planning his revenge. We had better look out.'

Samu was, indeed, planning his revenge and we soon found out what it was.

* * *

The place where we collected the water for our and Meyego's households was a long way down the hill. But the place was easy enough to get to from our house and it was the best part of the river for collecting water. There was a deep pool into which we dipped the containers and let them fill while we played a bit on the bank. There was a tree branch growing across the pool, around which we used to tie ropes to haul the heavy containers out of the middle of the pool with their clear water inside. We then swung the ropes to the bank with long sticks and the filling job was done. Of course, we still had to carry the containers all the way up the hill to the houses. But at least collecting nice, clean water was easy enough and quite fun.

We also had time to search for the wild spinach that grew near the river bank and which made such a difference to the normal non-taste of our porridge. Monica knew where the plants grew, and she made sure they were from the proper spinach plants, not from a different plant which looked the same, but tasted terrible and was poisonous.

Samu and his friends changed all this. The next time we went to collect the water, there was no deep pool. There was only a trickle of water running just above the bed of the river. Samu and his friends had destroyed the dam below the pool. They had rolled away the boulders that were blocking the stream and creating the pool. They had also cut away the logs and branches that had collected against the boulders making a good, watertight seal. This had kept the water level high and the pool nice and deep.

Now, it was going to take us ages to fill the containers. In order to fill them without getting any earth and mud in the water, we used small cups to take the water carefully from the surface of the trickle. We then emptied the contents of the cup carefully into the containers, making sure any mud stayed in the bottom of the cups. Before, when we had delivered containers with a little mud at the bottom to Meyego's compound, his wife shouted at us and told us to go back and collect some clean water.

That morning, it took us all day to collect clean water just for Meyego's household. We had to do without water at our household that day and go without any wild spinach. The next day, we managed to get better at scooping clear water from the top of the shallow stream, but it still took us much longer than before and there was never time to hunt for the spinach leaves, so we had to eat no-taste porridge from then on.

Samu had got his revenge.

As well as this, the prospect of us making time for Aiyasha to help us learn reading and writing and maths seemed more remote than it had been before.

'Were we going to have to stay dumb orphans for ever?' I asked myself that night, as I settled down on my mat and pulled the blanket over me.

Chapter 9

The trickle of an idea

The water collection work was beginning to get us down.

'There must be a better way of doing this,' said Luke. 'We must be able to find a better collection point. Today, I'm going to search along the river to find one.'

'I'll come with you,' said Langa, who always worked closely with Luke.

That left only me, Jabu and Sakhile to do the water collection, as Monica had joined Jacob up on the mountain with the cattle.

It had been a long, slow process to fill the water containers. When we got back to the hut, we were hoping to hear that Luke and Langa had found a more promising collection point.

'No luck,' said Luke. 'But we have found some pipes and we are working on a plan to use them instead of the cups. That should speed things up.'

Monica was back already. She had delivered the firewood to Meyego's wife and was placing some under our cooking pot.

Jacob was the last one back after herding the cattle into Meyego's kraal. Instead of slumping down onto the grass patch just below the stoep, as most of us did when we returned from the day's work, he strolled up to Aiyasha.

'Aiyasha,' he said, 'we are not using the glass jar to keep spinach leaves any longer. Can I use it, please, for my tadpoles?'

Jacob then took a plastic bag that he had tied onto his belt and showed it to us.

'Look at these tadpoles I have caught,' he said proudly. 'It will be very interesting to see how they develop. We need to give them plenty of fresh water and to feed them so they grow and change into frogs.'

Then he added, 'It will be important that we put some fresh water in each day so they survive.'

'OK,' said Aiyasha, 'you can use the spinach jar. We will all be interested to watch them develop.'

Then she added a little sternly, 'But on the understanding that when they do change into frogs, you let them go and don't keep them as pets. We don't want frogs all over the house.'

Jacob agreed and then asked if he could use some of the fresh water we had just brought back from the river to fill up the jar. We let him half fill the jar, because we were now bringing back less water from the river and we needed every drop for cooking, cleaning and washing ourselves.

You could see Sakhile had been thinking. She had that frown she wore whenever she was concentrating on something.

Rather slowly, Sakhile asked, 'Where did you find the tadpoles, Jacob? I thought you had been up on the mountain all day with the cattle?'

'Oh, yes,' said Jacob, 'I was.'

'But there is no water up on the mountain,' responded Sakhile. 'It's all in the river, in the bottom of the valley.'

'Well, it's not,' said Jacob with a superior look. 'Yesterday, I found a small trickle running beside the opening of the big cave. I dug a channel to take it away from the snake rock and led it to a hollow further down. This afternoon, when I went back, there was a small pool of water in the hollow and these tadpoles were swimming around in it.'

Then Aiyasha called out. 'Hey, you two. You are supposed to be on cooking fire duty. You can carry on your discussions about tadpoles later. If we don't get the fire lit under the cooking pot soon, it will be dark before the porridge is ready to eat. There is no moon tonight, so we need to get on with it.'

After we had eaten our plates of no-taste porridge, we sat around the dying flames of the fire, still feeling hungry, as we did every night. We were waiting for the last warmth of the fire to fade before getting ready to go to sleep.

Then, from the other side of the fire, Jabu spoke slowly. 'If there is water up on the mountain, wouldn't it be better if we got it from there? It would be so much easier and quicker carrying the full containers down the hill, than hauling them uphill as we do now.'

Nobody answered. But I could sense everyone thinking.

Everyone was thinking how marvellous it would be to be able to bring the water downhill instead of hauling it up. Although I could not see their faces in the dark, I knew everyone was smiling at the idea.

Then Langa said, 'But there's not enough water up there.' He paused, then added, 'If Jacob's trickle took a whole day to half fill a small hollow, how long will it take to fill just one container?'

'Langa is right,' said Jacob. 'But I'm thinking there must be more than a trickle. You see, for tadpoles you need frogs to lay eggs, and frogs lay eggs in ponds. I think there must be a pond higher up from which the trickle is coming. If we follow the trickle back, we may find the pond.'

'A little problem,' said Langa. 'You said the trickle was coming out of the mouth of the big cave. Is that the cave that is guarded by the cobras?'

'Yes,' answered Jacob. 'That is why I scraped the channel from the side of the entrance, to get as far away from the cobras as possible.'

There was a soft groan from around the fire. The excitement and hope retreated and disappeared into the distant darkness. Everyone knew that trying to get past the cobras would surely result in a deadly strike by one or more of them.

After a short silence, Jacob spoke again. 'I know how to get into the cave safely. I will go with Pele. The cobras won't come near if they see Pele is with me.'

'I agree,' said Sakhile. 'Pele will keep the cobras away. I will come with you.' Then she added, 'It will be dark in the cave, but I've got an idea how we may be able to bring some light with us to see our way. I'd like to try that out.'

Now we were excited again and began discussing the prospect of exploring the cave and hunting for the frog pond. The North Star was high in the sky before Aiyasha decided it was time to move into the hut and go to sleep.

I think, like me, most of us dreamt that night of exploring the cave and imagining what we might find, and what it might mean for our lives.

Chapter 10

Cave exploration

Sakhile had always been the curious one of the Bundu Bunch, so we called her the experimenter. She was always wondering and asking questions about the things she saw around her. For example, when we went to the river to fetch water, Sakhile noticed that some things floated and others did not. She was curious about what made something a floater or a sinker.

Langa said, 'That's simple. Wood floats and stone sinks. Look.' He threw a stick onto the water and we watched it float down the river. I then threw a stone into the middle of the river, and it sank to the bottom.

'See,' said Langa, 'some things are floating things and others are sinking things.'

'Yes, but why are some things floaters and others sinkers?' asked Sakhile.

'They just are,' said Langa.

Meyego's water containers were full by then, so she and Langa started back up the hill. I stayed to fill our own containers. As I did so, I did think a bit about what Sakhile had said and was not really satisfied with Langa's answer to Sakhile's 'why?' question.

Sakhile added to the mystery the next day. She brought a piece of wood from one of the ironwood trees growing in the forest. She asked us to watch as she threw the wood into the river. It sank to the bottom. Then she placed a stone on a dry leaf and the stone floated merrily downstream. Langa's 'they just are' response seemed even more unsatisfactory than before.

While I was thinking about Sakhile's stone–leaf puzzle, I heard Jacob asking her to tell him more about her idea of taking a light into the cave with them.

'This is the time of year that there are lots of lighting worms and flies,' she replied. 'If we catch some of them and put them into a glass jar, then we would have a lantern we could take with us into the cave. The lighting worms are by the river, but the lighting flies are mostly seen in the forest.'

Sakhile then went on to say, 'I will find some lighting worms down by the river this morning. There are lots at the pool where there are reeds and they are on the guava bushes, which are full of fruit right now.'

'OK,' said Jacob. 'What do I need to catch the lighting flies? I can get those from the forest before I come back this evening.'

'You will need some netting,' said Sakhile. 'That's how I caught some once, but I let them go as I didn't have a jar to put them in. You better take a jar with you to save the flies you catch.'

That evening, Jacob came back to the hut with a jar quite full of lighting flies. We saw the glow of the jar on the hillside before we saw him clearly. Sakhile said they needed to put her worms in the jar as well. She also put in some damp cloth and pieces of guava because she said the worms liked moist conditions and would eat the fruit.

After we had eaten outside by the cooking pot, Sakhile took the jar into the hut and it was amazing. The jar lit up one corner of the hut. As we settled down to sleep, we all kept looking at the jar to see how long it would continue glowing brightly. It was still glowing strongly as the last pair of eyes closed and the whole hut was fast asleep.

I woke early next morning, while it was beginning to get light. The first thing I did was to look for the lighting jar. There it was and it was still glowing. What a good start to the day. Everyone went off to their chores feeling pretty chuffed.

We left the lantern in the hut and it was still glowing as we went to sleep the next night. However, by the second morning, the lantern was no longer glowing. Sakhile took the lid off the jar and saw that the flies and worms had all died.

She then called the Bundu Bunch together and explained what we needed to do.

'We must not let the flies and worms die again,' she said. 'We must let them go before that happens.'

It was decided that Sakhile and Jacob would collect the worms and flies to make another lantern as quickly as possible that morning. They would then go to the cave with Pele and start exploring inside while the lantern was still glowing strongly. This meant that the others needed to work harder to do the water collection and cattle herding chores without their help.

It was also agreed that the worms and flies would be released at the end of the day.

* * *

As we had anticipated, doing the chores without Sakhile and Jacob needed more effort on the part of everyone else. So, at the end of the day, when we gathered back at the hut, we were all very tired. But we were also very excited to hear what Sakhile and Jacob had found in the cave.

Aiyasha insisted that we prepare and eat the porridge first and then, once we had finished eating and cleared up, we could gather around the cooking fire and listen to their story.

This is what they told us. Jacob began.

'We got to the cave and noticed the trickle was still coming from the side of the entrance. I took Pele from my coat pocket and held him in front of me as we approached the gaping cave mouth. As expected, a cobra slid out slowly from under one of the rocks. However, before it reared up to attack us, it must have noticed Pele because it slunk back again. We continued into the cave without seeing any more of the cobras.

'We had only gone a few steps into the cave, when it got very dark and very cold. Sakhile took the lantern from under her jumper and we could see a few feet in front of us. That was enough for us to negotiate the narrow tunnel, which seemed to be going gradually uphill. We noticed that one side of the channel was quite damp.

'The tunnel became narrower and the roof got lower. We had to crouch to avoid hitting our heads on the rock above us. Then the tunnel seemed to split into two. On the dry side it went upwards. On the damp side it continued at the same level. We continued along the dry side. We were very pleased to have the lantern with us, as we soon realised that we were on a ledge, with a bigger and bigger drop on what had been the damp side of the tunnel. Soon, we could no longer see to the bottom of the drop. Also, the ledge got narrower and narrower. We couldn't go on any further and I told Sakhile to turn round carefully so as not to fall over the side of the ledge.'

Sakhile then took up the story. 'I turned round, but the ledge was so narrow and the roof of the tunnel so low that I hit my elbow on the side of the rock and felt myself falling over sideways. I desperately felt for something to hold onto. My fingers found a crack on the rock surface and, as my foot went over the edge, I was able to pull myself back.

'That is when we heard it. A splash way below us. My foot had dislodged a small piece of the ledge and it had fallen over the edge into the darkness. And into water!

'We made our way slowly back down the incline of the ledge to where it got wider and we felt safe. I held the lantern over the edge, but we still couldn't see anything below. Luckily, that morning I had put on my warmer dress, which I wore with a string for a belt. I tied the string carefully around the top of the jar and gently lowered it down over the edge.

'I was nearly at the end of the string when a sparkle came up at us from below. By that time, Jacob had found a loose stone which he threw over the edge. We counted one, two, three, four … and then splash. And, from the lantern, we could see the shining ripple on the surface of the water.

'Jacob found another stone and threw it further out. That also made a splash, although we couldn't see anything this time. We then realised that there must have been a wide pool of water below us.

'We went back down to where the tunnel path had seemed to split. The damp side was flat, but the gap was tiny. There was no way we could get through it and follow the damp path. We made our way back to the cave opening.'

Sakhile finished by saying, 'So there actually is a pool of water in the cave, as Jacob suspected, and it must be quite large. Now we need to think how we can tap into it to fill our water containers.'

Then, with a smile, Jacob went on to tell us the end of his story. 'When we got to the mouth of the cave, the sunlight was blinding and, at first, we didn't see him. It took us a while to make out Pele's shape, sitting up and looking at us. He looked very pleased with himself. And then we saw why. In front of him was a dead cobra.

'I thought I had put Pele back in my coat pocket as we went into the cave. But he must have jumped out and gone hunting for cobras. While we were exploring the darkness, Pele was focusing on his next meal!'

By the time Sakhile and Jacob had finished their story it was late, and Aiyasha said we had to go to sleep. Before we went into the hut, Sakhile took the jar down the hill a little way and took off the lid. We watched as the lighting flies sparkled away and spread out into the night air. She then emptied the worms at the base of a low bush and we saw them climb among the leaves and light up the foliage.

We had made a wonderful discovery of a pool of water up on the mountain. But now we had to figure out if and how we could use it to reduce the time it was taking us to collect water from the shallow river bed. Even if we couldn't save much time, the prospect of saving our muscles by carrying the full water containers downhill instead of hauling them uphill seemed very attractive.

Chapter 11

The invention

Langa and Luke were always making things out of whatever they could find. They made cars with steering wheels out of wire and tin cans. They made windmills out of sticks and leaves. They made swings out of old tyres. They made catapults out of branches and inner tubes. They were the inventors of the Bundu Bunch.

One of the important things about inventors is knowing where to find the things you need to make your inventions. Langa and Luke knew their way around the places where the community dumped their rubbish, so they knew they would usually have no problem finding whatever they needed for an invention idea.

Before they started on their invention for using the water in the cave pool, they asked Sakhile to take them into the cave with another lantern. They saw that it was not possible to get through the gap directly to the pool. However, there was plenty of room to pass a pipe through the gap. They were not sure how far past the gap the pool began; however, they reasoned that, if they could find a pipe of about fifteen feet long, they may be able to push it to the edge of the pool. If so, the water from the pool would flow down the pipe.

They found a discarded pipe that was nearly as long as they wanted and went back to the cave. They were very excited as they pushed the pipe through the gap. They pushed and pushed until they had only a couple of feet left on their side of the gap. They were beginning to think they would need to come up with another plan, when they heard a gurgling noise from the pipe and water came gushing out. Lovely clear, cold water. They did high fives and gave a cheer. But then their feet got wet as the cave floor began to fill with water. They quickly pulled the pipe back out and the water flow stopped.

The two boys left the pipe in place, making sure no more water was coming from it. They were very pleased with themselves for solving the problem of how to get water from the cave pool. But when they reported back to the Bundu Bunch, they discovered that they had a bit more inventing to do.

* * *

Everyone agreed that Langa and Luke had come up with a very clever invention.

However, Monica wasn't so enthusiastic. 'I don't think it will be practical to use on a daily basis,' she said. 'If you think about it, lugging the full containers back along the narrow tunnel will be difficult, and doing it in the dark will result in lots of banged heads and scraped arms. I don't think I would be keen to do it.'

'But if you take the lantern, you can see where you are going,' replied Luke.

Sakhile objected to that idea. 'First, it takes a lot of time to collect the worms and lighting flies. And second, the lighting worms and flies are only around for two months of the year.'

'OK,' said Langa, 'what we may be able to do is to channel the water to the entrance of the cave. I don't think we will be able to find much more pipe very easily, but I know where there is plenty of old roof guttering we could use.'

'Brilliant,' said Monica. 'But someone would still need go deep into the cave every day to push the pipe into the pool, and then pull it out again when we have finished filling the containers. Would you need the lantern to do that?'

'It would be difficult without the lantern, and a bit scary,' Luke replied. 'Also, if it means going into the cave every day, we need to think about the risk from the cobras. We may not be able to rely on Pele every day. We know he goes off sometimes in the early mornings and only comes back at dusk.'

He thought for a moment. 'I've an idea how we may be able to control the pipe from outside the cave and avoid all these problems,' he continued. 'Langa and I will work on it and see if we can come up with a practical solution.'

Langa looked at Luke and together they gave us a thumbs up and said, 'CAN DO',

'*CAN DO*'. This was becoming our Bundu Bunch motto.

* * *

Their idea required a few additional materials. The item that gave them the most difficulty was finding enough rope. They needed enough to go from the mouth of the cave to the pool inside the cave, and enough extra to go to a tree further down the hill from the cave entrance. They were able to find some short pieces of rope at the dump sites, but not nearly enough. It was Monica who directed them to the place where they were able to obtain the rope they needed.

* * *

One evening, when they were talking around the fire and discussing the rope problem, Monica came up with an idea.

'Do you remember when they were laying the foundations of the new church building that is nearly finished now? The builders used rope to mark out where they needed to dig the foundation trenches. They used a lot of rope because they had to go all around the outside of the building. I noticed some rope lying with the pile of rubble and other building materials they had finished with.'

Langa and Luke went to the church the next day and saw a small section of rope sticking out from under a pile of building rubble. They pulled and more came out. They kept on pulling. In the end, they pulled out all the rope they needed and more. They coiled it up and carried it back to the orphan hut.

The other materials were easy to find. They included the roof guttering that Langa knew about, some heavy stones, a strong smooth tree branch and a section of tin roofing. Here's what they did with these items to make their invention.

They used the narrow gap in the cave in two ways. First, to wedge the pipe firmly in place on the floor of the cave tunnel with heavy rocks. The second use of the narrow gap was to wedge the section of the tree branch high up in the crack.

They tied one end of the rope and a heavy stone to the end of the pipe. Then they put the rope over the tree branch before they wedged the branch into place.

Now, when they pulled on the rope, it lifted the end of the pipe out of the water. When they released the rope, the heavy stone at the end of the pipe pulled it down into the water.

The rest was easy. They laid the guttering on the cave floor to carry the water from the end of the pipe. They used the tin roofing to make a funnel to take the water from the guttering into their containers.

Lastly, they attached the end of the rope to the tree outside the cave and pulled it tight.

Now, when they wanted water to fill the containers, they untied the rope from the tree and let it go slack. The end of the pipe in the cave dropped into the pool and, before long, water started to appear in the guttering, which they funnelled into the containers. When the containers were full, they tightened the rope to pull the end of the pipe out of the water, tied it to the tree and the water stopped flowing.

The invention worked. What's more, it was practical as it was not necessary to go up to the cave entrance or into the cave to get the pool water to flow into the containers.

When they demonstrated their invention to the rest of the Bundu Bunch, there was much cheering and high-fiving. Everyone agreed that Langa and Luke were the best inventers in the world.

Chapter 12

The deception plan

We learnt about the water in the cave and we invented a way to get as much as we needed safely into the containers. Everyone agreed that we would now be able to complete our water collection duties much more easily and much more quickly than before. This would free up time for other things. Monica said she would like to find more edible plants to make our porridge tastier. Luke and Langa said they would enjoy spending more time at the dumps. They were keen to find the parts they needed to generate enough power to make an old torch light up.

Aiyasha let us all talk about the things we would do if we could finish the water collection duties before midday.

'You asked me to help you learn to read and write,' she said, 'and to do sums because you didn't like Samu and his friends teasing you about being dumb. I said I would think about it. If you can finish the water collection by midday, then we could have classes in the afternoons.'

'That's a wonderful idea,' said Monica. 'We could use the schoolroom after Cebsile's classes have finished. By early afternoon, teaching is finished and the school is empty.'

Then Jabu did a very strange thing. She jumped up and shouted, 'NO! NO!!!'

Everyone was taken aback, because we all agreed with Monica that using the free time to learn writing and maths was indeed a wonderful idea. We relished the prospect of being able to answer the questions Samu and his friends teased us with.

We all stared at Jabu with questioning looks. Nobody said anything.

Then Jabu said, 'We must not do the lessons like that. We must do them in secret.' She looked at us for a moment. 'When Meyego sees that we have time for afternoon lessons, he will find out about our water discovery. He will take control of the water source for his own ends. He won't let the community have any say in how the water is used. He will say, as he often does, that the community is in his briefcase and he knows what is best for it. He will use his control of the water source to increase his power over the community, and he will most likely make community members pay him for using the water.'

After her long speech, Jabu sat down to let her words sink in. When she saw everyone nodding their heads, she knew that we agreed on the need to keep the water discovery and the writing and maths classes idea secret.

'We need to come up with a deception plan so that nobody thinks we are doing things any differently than before,' she added.

'The thing is,' I pointed out, 'we don't actually have to go to the river at all. Nobody knows where along the river we now collect water after Samu destroyed our usual place. We could be collecting it from anywhere along the river.'

'That's right,' said Langa. 'So, if people don't see us at the river, they will assume we are somewhere else along it.'

'What we need to do,' I said, 'is to set off as if we were heading for the river and then double back and go up to the cave.'

'Fine,' said Sakhile, 'but how do we prevent people from seeing us going up the mountain with empty water containers?'

Jabu came up with an idea of how we might be able to do this. 'We could use that donga on the other side of Meyego's compound.'

A donga is a deep gully created by storm waters. It has steep sides and nobody can see you at the bottom unless they are standing right on its edge. So, the plan we came up with was to collect Meyego's empty containers, head downhill and go into the donga, and then walk along it uphill instead of downhill to the river. We would repeat this at the end of the day with the full containers. We would climb out of the donga below Meyego's compound and people would think we had come from the river.

We were all quite pleased with this plan. But Jabu insisted on adding another element of deception. She said we must also take our own empty containers with us when we collected Meyego's. Also, she insisted we did not climb out of the donga until we were in the forest. That way, nobody would observe any of us taking the empty containers up the hill.

To ensure the deception worked, it was decided that those doing the cattle herding that day would fill the containers just below the cave. Usually, nobody came up to the part of the mountain where the cave was, but if they did, and they saw the herders by the cave, they would not think there was anything strange about it.

Just below the cave, we found a big bush where we were able to hide the containers if anyone came close. To reduce the risk of discovery further, two of us were put on lookout for any intruders while the containers were being filled. If we saw anyone in the area, we whistled to alert the herders and they would quickly hide the containers and make a big thing about shouting at the cows to move them on.

I knew of a clearing deep in the forest, away from paths, where Jacob and I had made a hide last year. The idea of the hide was to enable us to watch the animals and birds in the clearing without them seeing us. I enjoyed watching birds catch insects and worms and make nests. Animals also came close, either passing through the clearing or to find food. I saw small buck, rock rabbits, meerkats and others that neither Jacob nor I knew the names of.

Thinking of this hide, I said, 'I know where we can meet safely in the forest and where the herders can bring the full water containers. You remember where we made our lookout hide, Jacob? We should meet there.'

It was agreed, and the hide clearing became our secure meeting place.

Chapter 13

ABC: Aiyasha's Briefcase Class

We operated our new water collection system for three days and were pleased that the deception plan seemed to work. Nobody commented on our activities and our cave water discovery remained our secret.

With our new system, we were able to fill the containers and have them stored behind the hide by midday. We then took them to Meyego's compound and our hut later in the afternoon. On the third day, when we were gathered in front of the hide, Aiyasha came with her blanket and sleeping mat and briefcase.

'Today, we will start our classes,' she said. She laid the blanket and mat on the floor and asked us to sit on them. She arranged us in a semicircle and sat down in front of us. Then, she opened her briefcase and pulled out a thick book with 'ABC' in big letters on its cover.

Aiyasha pointed to the book. 'We are going to use this book to learn the letters of the alphabet and how to write them. We will then learn how to read words made from letters of the alphabet.'

Now we were very excited. At last, we were going to have proper lessons and would be able to answer Samu's teasing questions.

'Learning in our classroom here,' said Aiyasha, 'is going to be a challenge. We have just this one book. We have no pencils. We have no paper, no posters, no blackboard. But I think we have what we need most and that is the desire to learn. Am I right, do we all have that?

Of course, Aiyasha received a resounding *YES* from all of us.

'OK,' said Aiyasha, 'first we need to make some tools that will help us learn quickly.' Then she gave each of us a task.

'Langa and Luke,' she said, 'I want you to use the ABC book to make copies of each of the alphabet letters shown in the book with the wire you have used before to make cars and other inventions.

'Monica and Jacob, I want you to go to the church building site to get the slats from the wooden pallets that have been left there.'

Aiyasha asked Sakhile and me to go and fetch some fine, clean sand from the riverbed. She asked Jacob to find a supply of small, rounded pebbles and a dozen small sticks, and to sharpen the ends.

Aiyasha used the wood to make shallow boxes into which she put a layer of sand. She used the sharp sticks to draw letters in the sand. She called these our writing tablets. When we needed a new page, all we had to do was smooth over the sand and write some more.

Using the ABC book, the wire alphabet letters, the tablets and the stick pencils, we started to learn to read and write. Using the pebbles, we learnt to count and do sums.

We were hungry to learn and soaked up everything Aiyasha taught us like thirsty sponges. We might still be short of food to fill our bellies, but we now had plenty of material to fill our minds.

At Aiyasha's classes, we did not only learn how to read and write and do sums. Every day, Aiyasha would take out something different from her briefcase and we learnt to name it, spell the name and write it on our tablets. Also, Aiyasha would explain how each item fitted into our world and the world beyond. She might pull out a leaf. She would tell us which plant it came from and how it helped the plant to grow. She would tell us where in our valley the plant could be found and where else in the world we would find that plant. Sometimes, she pulled out the ABC book and pointed to animals, birds, buildings, cities and people and told us about them.

Each morning, at about midday, Aiyasha would call out 'ABC time' and we all gathered on the mat in front of the hide, eager to learn something new. When Aiyasha called out, I think she had the ABC book in her mind. However, we came to think of ABC as meaning 'Aiyasha's Briefcase Class'.

* * *

Early on, at the end of one of the briefcase classes, Jabu stood up and gave us one of her serious looks. She asked us if we were pleased to be learning so much. Of course, we all enthusiastically confirmed that we were.

Then Jabu responded by saying, 'This is because our deception plan is working well. We have not been disturbed because nobody knows about ABC. If Meyego gets to know we are gaining so much knowledge, he will find out how and he will not be pleased that something is happening in the community that is not under his control. He will put a stop to it all.

'That is why we must keep the deception going. This means not letting anyone guess that we are learning to read and write and do sums. However tempting it may be to stop Samu's teasing by showing him we can write our names and do maths, we must keep up the impression that we don't know anything. We must continue to pretend that we are dumb.'

We all saw the sense in what Jabu said. At first, I was a bit disappointed to think that we must not demonstrate our new skills, or let anyone know how much we were learning, but then I began to realise that the idea of keeping our secret was quite appealing. I even began to think that I could enjoy Samu's teasing when I knew it wasn't true and that we knew something that he did not!

Chapter 14

Exposure

I suppose it had to happen. It was too much to expect that our deception would go undiscovered forever.

It was a Wednesday. Aiyasha was telling us about the four rocky planets. She had taken four round pebbles from her briefcase and placed them in a row by a large rock at one side of the clearing. The pebble nearest the big rock was Mercury. It was the smallest of the four pebbles. Then came Venus, then Earth, then Mars. These three pebbles were all about the same size. Aiyasha explained how all these planets moved in circles around the big rock, which was the sun. Mercury was closest to the sun, and it took three months to go right round. Venus was next closest, taking six months, the Earth took a whole year and Mars took two years. We were quite excited as we made plans to look for our neighbouring planet, Mars, that evening. Aiyasha said we would be able to see it high in the night sky shortly after sunset.

The excitement was shattered when Samu jumped out from behind the hide and shouted gleefully, 'Caught you!'

With a satisfied smile on his face, he said, 'I knew you lot were up to something, because none of us has seen much of you about in the valley these past few weeks.' Looking around, he went on. 'So this is where you come. Trying to get some knowledge into your dumb heads, I see.'

And then he said, 'I also see that you have the full water containers behind the hide. That's interesting. I think I will do some investigating to see where you are filling them from.'

With that, he gave us another smile and started to head up the hillside, towards the cave.

We all looked at each other with crestfallen faces.

'Quick, we better stop him from finding the cave,' said Luke, making a move to the edge of the clearing.

'I'll come with you,' said Langa, 'but I'm not sure how we are going to persuade him to go somewhere else.'

Sakhile said, 'If he finds it, do you think we should tell him everything and beg him to keep our secret?'

'Yes, maybe,' I said. 'But what can we offer him in return?'

Just after Luke and Langa left the clearing, we heard a terrified scream from higher up the mountain.

'Oh, no!' said Monica. 'Samu must have found the cave – and the cobras.'

'Quick,' said Jabu, looking at Jacob. 'Go to the cave as fast as you can and take Pele with you.'

Jacob grabbed Pele and scrambled up the hill as fast as he could. He found Samu standing with his back hard against the rock at the side of the cave entrance. He looked terrified. His hands were holding his head and his eyes were bulging with fright. He was staring at two cobras rearing up in front of him.

In a calm voice, Jacob spoke slowly. 'It's OK, Samu. I've got Pele with me, he will save you. Just stay very still.'

Jacob then took Pele from his pocket and pointed him at the two cobras. Pele darted straight at the closest cobra. The cobra struck at him, but Pele twisted to his side and bit the cobra's head as it came down next to him. Then he darted away again. Both cobras were now focused on Pele, who was darting in and out between them.

Jacob went to Samu's side. He still had not moved. He was staring straight ahead. Then he started shaking. Jacob helped him move away from the rock face.

As Jacob took Samu's arm around his neck and began to guide him down the hill, he said, 'It's OK, Samu, you are safe now.' Samu continued to stare ahead and didn't say a word.

Luke and Langa came to help and, between them, they carried and dragged Samu to the ABC clearing. They sat him on the mat. Still Samu was staring ahead without seeming to see anyone and he didn't say anything. He was just shaking and shaking.

'Samu is in shock,' said Aiyasha. 'It will take a while for him to recover.'

Aiyasha then took the blanket we had been sitting on and wrapped it around Samu's shoulders. Slowly, the shaking became less and Samu began to relax.

Meanwhile, Jacob had gone back up the hill to where he had left Pele skirmishing with the cobras. When he got there, they were still at it, but the cobras seemed to be getting slower and slower. Jacob told Pele to stop and went to pick him up. Pele, however, was intent on continuing until he had killed both the snakes and he jumped away from Jacob.

'NO! I said STOP,' said Jacob in a much sterner voice. Pele looked at him with large, pleading eyes, but came away and let Jacob pick him up and put him in his pocket. The two snakes slid away under the warm rocks at the side of the cave mouth.

When Jacob got back to the clearing, he found Samu had stopped shaking and staring ahead and Aiyasha was helping him to his feet. He looked around at all of us and then slowly walked to the edge of the clearing and into the forest, heading downhill towards his father's compound. He still hadn't said a word.

* * *

In the evening, we identified the planet Mars as a steady bright light in the night sky where Aiyasha said it would be. But the excitement and wonder at seeing our neighbouring planet were dampened by the events of that afternoon.

Chapter 15

The scholarship competition

The next day, Aiyasha called 'ABC time' and we gathered on the mat and blanket as usual. But we were not as attentive as usual.

Our minds were on the consequences of Samu's discovery of our secret and we worried that our deception had been exposed. We expected that, at any moment, we would hear footsteps coming up the hill and Meyego's booming voice calling out, 'Urgh, Aiyasha! Where are my orphans?'

But it didn't happen that day, or the next, or the next.

After a week or so, we began to relax and things went back to how they had been before Samu's visit. Or, almost as they had been. Two things were different.

First, the classes got better and better. Aiyasha started to pull out different books from her briefcase. There were more pictures to talk about, and she began to read us stories about animals and people and what happened to them. She also started to give us books to read ourselves.

I did wonder a bit about how Aiyasha's briefcase could hold so many books. But in the story books I had been reading, there were magical things with special properties. I told myself that this must be a special, bottomless briefcase. I didn't have time to worry too much about this mystery, for I was enjoying the new-found worlds revealed in the books. At that time, you would see us members of the Bundu Bunch with a book in our hand, while we did the chores or walked back to the hut in the evenings.

The second thing that was different was that Aiyasha finished her briefcase classes earlier than before. She told us she was giving us time to stay at the clearing and do our own reading before it was time to take the water and firewood to the homesteads and the cattle to the kraals. We were more than happy to have an extra half-hour reading time.

On an evening about six months after Samu's visit, Aiyasha called us together outside the orphan hut after we had all returned from our chores. She had a glint in her eyes and the hint of a smile on her face as she told us what had happened that afternoon after she left us in the forest clearing.

She told us to sit down and listen up. And this is what she said.

'I was walking on the road that goes past the school, when a big car stopped next to me. In the car were three white people. The driver asked for directions to Meyego's compound. I told them they had to turn off the road onto a narrow track on the left, just after the big avocado tree. I told them that when they came to a fork in the track they needed to take the wider track, and then look for a turn to the right.

'Because they still seemed a bit worried about getting lost, I offered to go with them and show them the way. I climbed into the back seat. The lady at the front told me their names. The driver was Philip and she was Lorna. I can't remember the other one. They explained they were from an international donor organisation and were here to implement a scholarship programme for a selected number of children in each community.

'I learnt that, in each community, children aged five to seven would compete to be selected to receive the scholarships which will pay for schooling through primary school and high school. There would be a writing, reading and maths test. The ten children who did best in the test would be awarded the scholarships.

'The lady called Lorna told me that the headman of each community had been asked to call a community meeting to announce the scholarship programme and ask all families to provide the names of eligible children they would like to compete. Lorna said they were here to collect this list from the headman.

'I told Lorna that I was sure there had not been a community meeting in Bundami, and that households like ours had not been invited to submit names for the scholarship competition. The driver, Philip, then confirmed that there had been no community meeting in Bundami. He said that in Bundami the headman had said there was no need to waste time on a community meeting as he had all the information required in his briefcase.'

Aiyasha went on. 'Before Philip had finished talking, I was writing down your names. I gave the list to Lorna and asked her please to add your names to the list they collect from headman Meyego. Lorna took the list and told me that she would do so, and that you must come to the community school next Monday to take the test. She said each of you must bring a pencil with you.

'By this time, we were approaching Meyego's compound. I pointed it out and asked if I could be dropped off before they got there. I got out of the car and watched it drive up the narrow track into Meyego's compound.'

Aiyasha finished her story by saying, 'This is your chance to get a proper education. It will give you orphans an equal opportunity to get jobs, and do as well as other luckier children whose parents can pay to send them to school.'

We could understand why Aiyasha looked so excited and more animated than we had ever seen her before. She said this was our chance to do well for ourselves. But I figured it was also the chance for us to reward Aiyasha for everything she had done for us.

I am sure all of us resolved to do our best at the test, not only for our own sakes but for Aiyasha's sake, as well.

Sakhile interrupted my thoughts. 'But, what about the pencils?'

Everyone wondered what she was on about.

'Lorna told you we must all bring pencils,' Sakhile continued. 'We don't have any. We just have our sticks, and I don't think we will do very well in the test with sticks instead of pencils.'

Aiyasha said, 'Of course you are right, Sakhile. Tomorrow, I will get pencils for us all and also some paper. You will have the next two days to practise writing with pencils and paper instead of sticks and sand.'

And practise we did.

Chapter 16

The test

I woke up early on the day of the test, just as it was getting light. I woke with mixed feelings. I felt excited about taking the test, but I also felt a little concerned. I was worried about whether we would really be allowed to participate and also that we may not do well.

As the dawn light crept into the hut, I noticed Aiyasha standing in the doorway, looking out at our valley. My feelings turned to gratitude, admiration, love and awe for this girl who had done so much for us. That led to a feeling of determination and resolve. We would take the test, we would win a scholarship and we would make the most of our opportunity to succeed in the world. And, someday, we would repay Aiyasha for all she had done for us.

The others began to stir and stretch out.

Aiyasha turned round. 'Time to get up,' she said. 'It's test day today. As it is a special day, we will have some porridge before you go to the school. I want to make sure you stay alert through the test.

'Langa and Luke, please light the cooking fire. Monica and Sakhile, you can wash first. But everyone must use less than half a jug of water today as the porridge will take a full jug and there won't be enough for everyone if we all use our usual half jug for washing.

'Jabu and Sipho, please roll up the mats and blankets and then start heating the water in the pot for the porridge.

'Jacob, when you are washed and dressed, please go to Meyego's compound and tell someone there that you will be coming for the cattle later today, and that the cows must be kept in the kraal until you come. And you can bring their empty water containers back here.'

This was a change to our normal routine and it was the first time ever that Aiyasha was going to feed us before we set off on our daily chores. But, of course, it was the first time ever that we were going to the community school to do a scholarship test.

It felt strange eating a meal first thing in the morning, but it was very welcome and added to the realisation of what a special day this was going to be. Before we left for the school, Aiyasha gave us each a pencil and also some advice.

'Enjoy this special day,' she said. 'Enjoy having the opportunity to show people what you know and what you can do. You have worked hard and it has been difficult to keep your learning a secret for so long. Keep calm and make sure you listen well to the instructions and read any written questions carefully, then have fun answering them. Good luck.'

With that advice ringing in our ears and a bespoke breakfast bulging Bundu Bunch bellies, we set off down the hill to the community school. As we went we repeated our motto softly to ourselves: *CAN DO, CAN DO.*

When we approached the school, we saw two big cars and Meyego's truck outside. There were six or seven white people talking to Meyego. These people were obviously from the international donor organisation. They had a pile of notebooks with them and were showing them to Meyego.

There was a line of children in front of the schoolroom door, waiting to go in. We saw Samu there. This was the first we had seen of him since his cobra scare. He noticed us, but looked away. He obviously did not want to greet us.

We joined the end of the line. Meyego's sister, Cebsile, was at the door letting one child in at a time. She checked their names on her list and checked to see if they had a pencil with them before she let them into the classroom.

When Monica got to the front of the line, Cebsile looked at her crossly.

'What are you doing here?' she said. 'You are not on the list.' Then, looking at the rest of us, she added, 'Why are you not collecting our water and tending Meyego's cows?'

In a friendly manner and with a smile, Jabu said, 'It's OK, teacher. You see, Aiyasha arranged with the donor lady for us to be included on the list.'

Cebsile looked cross as she told us to wait at the side and dealt with the last three children who had arrived after us. Then she strode over to where the donor people were talking with Meyego.

There was a discussion between Meyego and Cebsile, which included a lot of shaking of heads. With his big rolling strides, Meyego came over to us.

'Urgh, you orphans are not included,' he said. 'This is only for children who know their letters and their numbers. Your job is to fetch water and herd the cattle. Go back at once and get on with the work you are supposed to be doing. I will speak to Aiyasha about this later.'

He then turned around and swaggered back to the donor group. He didn't notice Monica following right behind him. When they got up to the group, Monica said in a loud voice, 'Can I speak to Lorna, please?'

Meyego whipped around with a look of fury. He was not used to his instructions being disobeyed.

'Go back and get on with your work, this minute!' he shouted, and pointed to us, 'And take all those dumb orphans with you.'

Listening to this, I thought, 'Well done, Monica, brave try. But it seems we don't get to do the test, after all.'

One of the men in the donor group turned to Meyego. 'Hang on, Mr Meyego,' he said. 'Did that girl mention the name Lorna? And did you say orphans?'

Then he turned to the whole group. 'Lorna had to go to a meeting with the Head of Delegation this morning. But she mentioned to me that she had met a member of an orphan group last week and had agreed they could take the test.'

He looked at our group of orphans and then continued. 'Lorna was going to bring the list of names she had been given, but she was asked to attend the meeting just as she was about to leave.'

Then he asked the others, 'Did Lorna give her list to any of you?'

There was no answer.

'OK,' said the donor man, 'Lorna may make it here later. In the meantime, I propose we let the orphan group take the test, as they are here now and I see they all have their pencils ready.'

Meyego's face was getting redder and redder.

'No!' he said. 'I am the headman of Bundami community and I decide what happens here.'

Then he opened his briefcase and took out a sheet of paper with a list of names written on it. He waved it at the donor group.

'This is the community list of children to take the test, and these dumb orphans are not on this list.'

'With respect, Mr Meyego,' said the donor man quietly, 'we are providing the scholarships, and we have a duty to our donors to ensure the scholarships are distributed fairly.'

He went on, 'Furthermore, as I understand it, there was no community meeting in Bundami to inform everyone of the scholarship opportunity. Lorna told these orphans they could take the test and that is how it will be.'

Then Cebsile, who had come from the schoolroom, spoke up. 'But these children have not paid for schooling, so they do not deserve to take the test. They know nothing, anyway.'

'In that case,' said the donor man, 'they will not win any of the scholarships.'

That seemed to satisfy Meyego and we were allowed into the schoolroom, where we were shown the desks to sit at.

The donor people came in and gave everyone a book, which had questions on one side of each page and space to write the answers on the other. The side with questions had writing and pictures and numbers. There were quite a lot of pages.

The donor man who had argued with Meyego explained that we had one hour to do the test. We didn't have to answer all the questions, but should do as many as we could. He explained that the other donor people would be in the classroom and that, if anyone did not understand a question, they should raise their hand and one of the donors would try to help.

I can't remember much about all the questions. All I know is that they were quite interesting and the pictures made it easy to understand them. It was really fun being able to write what we knew on paper and in a book. I had just reached the last question when the donor man banged on his desk and said the time was over. I couldn't believe a whole hour had gone by so quickly.

The other donor people collected the books. We were the last to be let out of the classroom. Samu and his friends were sitting on the grass where Cebsile was giving them something to eat. Each had a plate with a thick slice of bread liberally spread with peanut butter. Next to each slice of bread was a big, beautiful bun! We walked past with our mouths watering, craving for just one more bite on the crusty, custard-cream coating we remembered so well.

As we walked past, Samu took a big bite out of his bun and gave us a wink and a thumbs-up. Climbing back up the hill, Langa expressed our combined thoughts.

'What was that all about?' he said. 'Was Samu gloating at us about his revenge for our bun raid? Was he thanking us for saving him from the cobras? Or was he suggesting he did well in the test and would win a scholarship?'

Bright futures

It was midday by the time we left the school. We still had our work to catch up on. Jacob and Luke went to release Meyego's cattle from their kraal and take them to the grazing lands up on the mountain. Monica and Jabu went back to the orphan hut to get the empty water containers. Langa and I went into the forest to collect firewood. Sakhile went to the cave mouth to check that our water delivery invention was working. She then helped Monica and Jabu fill the containers and take them to the back of the hide.

When we finished our assignments and were gathered in the ABC clearing, Aiyasha said there was no time for a class. She asked us to tell her about the test instead.

Monica told Aiyasha about Cebsile telling us we could not do the test as we were not on her list.

'I was furious,' said Monica. 'I couldn't believe we had come so far and worked so hard only for Meyego to deny us the one chance to have an equal opportunity with the others. I didn't really think about it as I followed behind him. I was shaking a bit, whether with fury or fright I'm not sure; both I think. But I felt we had to speak up for ourselves for once.'

She paused, then said, 'When the donor man spoke on our behalf, I wanted to hug him with relief.'

Aiyasha smiled. 'I'm really proud of you, Monica, for being so brave and assertive. What did you all think about the test?'

I said, 'I really enjoyed doing it and the hour went by very fast. The bit I liked best was the writing question, which asked us to write the title of a story and the first ten lines of it. My title was "Swimming under a waterfall".'

'Yes, me too,' said Jabu. 'My title was "The mountain leopard and the long-ago people".'

'Me too,' said Sakhile. 'My title was "Lighting fly lanterns".'

'Me too,' said Langa. 'My title was "How to find Mars".'

'Me too,' said Monica. 'My title was "Leaves for a tasty relish".'

'Me too,' said Jacob. 'My title was "Mongoose meets snake".'

'Me too,' said Luke. 'My title was "Mountain water sources".'

'Gosh, Luke,' said Monica. 'I hope you didn't tell them where our cave pond was?'

'Don't worry,' replied Luke. 'My ten lines began by explaining that water sources on mountains couldn't possibly exist.' He gave a wink and a smile. We all laughed.

'Well done everyone for enjoying the test so much,' said Aiyasha with a broad smile. 'I'm proud of you all.'

Then Aiyasha told us that Lorna had said the names of the children who had won scholarships would be given to the headmen in each community two days after the test. That would be Wednesday.

The next day, Aiyasha did not hold her briefcase class. She said we could have the afternoon to ourselves. You can imagine what each of us did. Monica went down to the river to look for herbs to add to the porridge pot that night. Jacob took Pele up the mountain to hunt for Pele's supper. Langa and Luke went back to the dumps to find parts for their electric motor. Sakhile sat down in the clearing with a science book. I don't know what experiment she was reading about. Jabu took a walk to the top of the mountain and did her quiet thing. She called it contemplation. I took up my pencil and sat down to write the final chapter of this book. I couldn't finish it, of course, because the last chapter had not yet played out.

* * *

Wednesday came and we did our chores as usual. We noticed that Aiyasha had gone down the road leading to Meyego's compound.

We gathered back at the forest clearing, expecting Aiyasha to call out 'ABC time' as usual. But Aiyasha was not there. After waiting for ten minutes, we heard voices from below coming towards us.

Into the clearing came Aiyasha and a white lady. Aiyasha told us to sit on the mat in front of her and the lady, who she introduced as Lorna. Lorna stood up and smiled at us.

'I have come here for two reasons,' she said. 'First, to tell you how you did in the test and, second, to find out how you managed to do so well. First, I can tell you that all seven of you have been awarded a scholarship. In the Bundami community, we have awarded three other scholarships, to Elisa, David and to Samu. Congratulations on your success.'

Lorna continued, 'I have learnt how your success owes much to the resourcefulness and ingenuity of your teacher, as well as assistance from a surprising source. You all know how Aiyasha managed to teach you to read and write and do sums by using what she could find around you, and the ABC book in her briefcase. You probably don't know how the contents of Aiyasha's briefcase expanded so much in the last six months.'

She paused and looked at each one of us before continuing. 'You, unknowingly, were responsible for this. You saved Samu from the cobra attack. Samu was so grateful to you for having saved his life, that he resolved to help you. He arranged with Aiyasha to meet her in the forest every afternoon with the books she asked him to borrow from his school.'

Lorna finished by saying, 'I am very glad to have met you. I look forward to supporting you and seeing more of you as you progress through primary and secondary school. I know you will all do very well, because you have managed to win these scholarships despite living under very difficult circumstances. Well done and good luck.'

With that, Lorna gave each of us a high-five, waved goodbye and started down the hill.

Wow! What a surprise. Samu is our friend and not our arch enemy. Good old Samu. We now know what his wink and thumbs-up after the test was all about. There and then, we voted Samu as the second-best friend of the Bundu Bunch. Of course, you know who the first best friend is. She is at the edge of the clearing, saying goodbye to Lorna.

'How ironic,' I thought to myself. 'It was Meyego's son who enabled Aiyasha's briefcase to become bottomless, and thereby have such a positive influence on our lives.' I remembered the dream I had had the first night in the orphan hut, about the two briefcases. Meyego's smart new briefcase and Aiyasha's old battered briefcase. I smiled to myself, now knowing how the dream must have ended.

That evening, we were all very quiet as we sat around the fire, deep in our own thoughts. The light from the dying flames faded away and I looked up at the inky night sky. I saw Mars in its usual place, playing its small but important part among the millions of bright stars piercing the blackness and infinite space of the universe. This made me think of my place and my part in the world.

It was reassuring to think that I was part of something so wondrous and vast, and that I had a tiny but important part to play in it. As I looked at all the bright twinkling stars, I realised that I could have, and resolved that I *would* have, an equally bright future.

In my dreams that night, I was swimming under the waterfall. The bubbles were the stars and the stars took on the form of old battered briefcases. My doubts about my future were gone, anything seemed possible.

BOOK II

Aiyasha's Appeal

Contents

Chapter 1

A busted ego

The hut seemed lifeless. For the three years I had been living at the orphan hut, I had become used to having seven older children around me. I was five years old when that changed and the laughter and chatter of the Bundu Bunch, as they called themselves, did not fill my days any more. I felt empty like the hut.

Aiyasha said, 'Buck up, Elah, they will be back soon for the holiday. We should be happy that they are attending classes at last. Just think of all the stories they will have for you when you see them next.'

Aiyasha is the 17-year-old head of our orphan family. We live in the orphan hut at the far end of the Bundami valley. Aiyasha is like a mother to me and the Bundu Bunch. But she is more than a mother, she is also a big sister and a best friend to all of us. I knew that she was putting on a good face for my sake. I could sense that she was not as at ease as she tried to make out.

And I knew the cause of Aiyasha's unease. It was Meyego, the headman of our Bundami community.

Meyego was getting very cross. He was more than cross. His ego had been punctured.

'I don't want to hear any more talk about ABC in Bundami,' Meyego instructed a group of parents who had come to see him about school places for their young children.

But talk there continued to be about what the community called 'the ABC', or Aiyasha's Briefcase Classes. The Bundu Bunch had attended these classes and had won seven out of the ten scholarships offered by an international donor to support children through primary and secondary school.

Meyego kept being asked by the other parents, 'What are you going to do to get ABC for our children?'

Of course, he could not give them an answer. He had no idea how to teach children to read, write and do sums. His sister, Cebsile, ran the local community school. But out of thirty of her pupils who had done the scholarship test, only three had won scholarships. Cebsile was not a good teacher. All she did was copy words from her textbook onto the blackboard and get the pupils to learn by repeating the words together over and over again.

Meyego felt humiliated because he expected to be able to tell his people what to do. Indeed, he revelled in telling them exactly what they must do and what they must not do.

To compound his humiliation, Aiyasha had overridden Meyego's idea of how to use the cave water source that the orphans had discovered on the hills above the homesteads. Once he had learnt of the spring on the mountain, Meyego made plans to put in a pipeline to his homestead and offer to sell water to those who could pay.

Aiyasha had a different plan. She had spoken to the donor lady, Lorna, who had agreed to let her orphan pupils take the scholarship test. Lorna listened to Aiyasha's water plan and had agreed that the donor would buy lots of pipes and lots of taps so that each group of three households could share a standpipe and tap, which would be no more than 100 metres from each home. And nobody would have to pay for the water from the standpipe.

The community members were now talking about not only ABC, but also APP (Aiyasha's pipeline plan). It was now more common to see groups of community members outside our orphan hut than outside Meyego's compound.

That night, as I lay on my mat and Aiyasha put the blanket over me, I said, 'Aiyasha, Meyego is not going to do something bad to us, is he?'

Aiyasha replied, 'I think he is cross with me right now and he doesn't like people coming to me instead of him, especially as I am a girl and only seventeen years old. But don't worry, he will probably get over it.'

Then she hugged me and said, 'There is nothing he can do to make things worse for us. I don't mind what he does, as long as he doesn't prevent the Bundu Bunch from continuing with their schooling, and the donor scholarship will ensure that cannot happen.'

She smiled and gave me a kiss. 'Goodnight. Dream about what you will do with the Bundu Bunch on their next holiday. It's only six weeks away now.'

* * *

The Bundu Bunch. Monica, so good at finding and using plants for our benefit. Sakhile, so probing with her questions about how things work. Jacob, who seemed to be able to talk with animals. Jabu, so good at organising and coordinating the actions of everyone. Luke and Langa: was there nothing they could not make or mend? And Sipho, the mimic and joker who bonds the Bundu Bunch with fun stories of their exploits. They didn't feature just in my dreams. I thought about them all the time. I wished I had a talent that matched theirs. I looked up to them with admiration and awe. I was always going to be looking up to them.

Chapter 2

Throwing the bones

I lived for the holidays. When the Bundu Bunch cousins all came back, the hut became alive again. They had so much to talk about. About their school, the schoolmasters and mistresses. About the other children and about their lessons. We talked late into the night around the cooking fire and under the starry sky. Aiyasha let me stay up to listen to accounts of what they got up to at the school and how they played tricks on their grumpy old maths teacher. Best of all were the stories of how Jacob managed to keep his pet mongoose, Pele, with him. Pele did get Jacob into trouble sometimes, but together the orphans managed to keep Pele a secret from the teachers. From time to time, they managed to divert blame for the damage Pele had done onto other children, especially those they didn't like very much.

What I enjoyed most were the times we spent together each day after we had done the chores. For the first time, they let me go with them on their exploration of the countryside around us. I learnt so much during those holidays. I learnt about plants and animals and insects and birds. And I learnt how to swim.

Sipho was my teacher.

'Elah,' he said when they first took me with them to the waterfall pool a year ago. 'Put your face under the water, open your eyes and blow bubbles, and imagine you are in a new world.'

It was as he said. I could easily imagine myself in a new world as I looked at the bubbles I was blowing under the water.

'But,' I said as I came up for air, 'I'm still standing. I'm not swimming.'

'Take your feet off the ground next time and you will be swimming,' Sipho assured me. And so I was. Now I was exploring those new underwater worlds.

In those happy days, I also learnt how a group with so many shared experiences could bond together so strongly and do so much for each other. In those holidays, I spent a lot of time with the Bundu Bunch. Yet, however much I yearned to do so, I never became a member of the Bundu Bunch. I just didn't have enough shared experiences. Besides, I knew I didn't have any of their talents and couldn't match their achievements.

* * *

When the holidays finished and the Bundu Bunch went back to school, life seemed to collapse into an empty existence again. After their third holiday, it was worse than this because things were becoming very difficult for Aiyasha and, therefore, for me as well.

As Aiyasha had thought, headman Meyego's busted ego did become a problem for us. In order to recover his self-esteem and authority in the community, he needed to discredit Aiyasha. To do this, he hatched up a two-step plan.

Step one. Make the people think that there is someone in the community who is causing them to suffer a hardship. In my community, this is not difficult as people believe in evil spirits and will look for an evil spirit to explain any hardship. They call the person who has an evil spirit in them a witch.

Meyego stopped bringing food back from the city and selling it cheaply to the community. People had to buy more expensive food from the shops and stalls, which meant that those with little money went hungry. Meyego explained that the city bakery and supermarkets who had previously given him the food for orphans had been told there were no longer any orphans in Bundami. That was why they were giving their spare food to other communities.

Meyego called a meeting and asked, 'Who has put a spell on the shop managers to make them think we do not need any food in Bundami?'

Step two. Make the community believe that Aiyasha was the cause of the food shortage problem. This also was not difficult. Meyego knew the Sangoma in the region. A Sangoma is a person with special powers that enable him or her to communicate with the ancestral spirits. He is able to divine the cause of people's problems by speaking to the ancestors and throwing bones. He then reads the bones to see what the ancestors are saying about who has the evil spirit that is causing the problem.

Meyego called the heads of all the families to his compound and asked them to sit in a circle around the Sangoma. The Sangoma had his jars of potions, his basket of spells, his boiling pot and his bag of bones with him. He picked up his bag of bones and waved it around his head as he communicated with the ancestors in a strange language. Then he opened the bag and threw the contents onto a mat in front of him.

While he continued chanting, he moved the bones around and around with a stick. Eventually, he picked out one bone and moved it away from all the rest. He pointed to the bone. Then he slowly looked around the circle of household heads.

'Our ancestral spirits have told me to pick out the smallest bone from the youngest animal,' he said. 'They are saying that the evil spirit is in the youngest of you. Show me who that is.'

Everyone pointed to Aiyasha.

Chapter 3

The playground project

Miss Gooday was committed to 'doing good'. She was also the senior teacher at Petranians College for Girls, Newcastle, England – or Petra for short. Each year, she organised a trip for her sixth-form girls to what she called 'a needy overseas community'.

This year, she had chosen the Bundami community for the 'doing good' trip. The idea was for the girls to design and build a playground at the community school. The previous term, they had been asked to draw plans for the playground and to approach their parents for the money needed for the project. This included the hire of an overland truck and living expenses to cover the cost of the six-week trip. Luckily, all the girls who went to Petra college had rich families and most of them gladly paid for their girls to 'have the experience of a lifetime', as Miss Gooday put it. Many parents were more than happy to pay the costs of the trip, if only to avoid having to put up with their teenage daughters moping around the house with their faces in their smartphones through the long summer holidays.

After travelling for two weeks, the girls arrived in the Bundami valley, where they were going to stay for a week. The community had prepared an area where they could pitch their tents and had also built a wooden shelter where they could cook. The girls met Cebsile and some of the parents of the schoolchildren. Then they put up their tents, and began to look for the poles and bolts and string and cement they would need to build the playground structures.

Two friends in the sixth-form group, Olivia and Audrey, didn't take this 'do-gooding' stuff too seriously. They were more interested in having a 'good time' than 'doing good'. They were much more interested in the people in the community and how they lived, than in digging holes and building anything. They spent their day walking all over the Bundami valley and, wherever they saw a group of people gathered, they would go up to them and start asking questions about how they managed without electricity, how they got their food, how they cooked, how they got their hot water, how they washed and ironed their clothes, who was in charge and so on. They also took lots of pictures of the people and their surroundings.

In this way, they learnt about the two orphans in the orphan hut at the far end of the valley. What was most appealing for the friends was that some people referred to the eldest orphan as a witch. It was not easy to get the people to explain why this girl, Aiyasha, was a witch, or what that meant or what her powers were. What they did hear was that some people thought that, following tradition, she would be poisoned so that her evil spirit would be killed with her.

Olivia and Audrey were keen to find out more and to meet an actual witch. They could not resist taking a complete day off from digging and make the long walk to the end of the valley to pay a visit to the 'witch hut'. When they got to the hut, they saw me helping Aiyasha to clean the cooking pot. I was pouring water from a tin into the pot that Aiyasha was scrubbing.

'Sanibonani, ninjani,' the girls called cheerily as they approached us. Olivia and Audrey had learnt this greeting of 'hello, how are you both' from the groups they had been talking with.

'Sikhona, siyabonga,' (we are fine, thank you) replied Aiyasha.

Aiyasha invited the girls to join us by the cooking pot and she brought out a mat for all of us to sit on. Olivia and Audrey introduced themselves and explained they were part of the Petra sixth-form group and that they were building the playground for the community school.

Olivia said suddenly, 'You don't look like a witch. You seem very nice and friendly.'

Aiyasha then told the two girls the whole story of why some in the community were calling her a witch.

'That's terrible,' said Audrey when Aiyasha had finished. 'What are you going to do about it?'

Aiyasha explained there was not much she could do. She hoped that, if she kept away from most people, they would forget about it as other things became more important to them.

That is when Audrey told Aiyasha that some people in the community were saying that she would be poisoned, so as to kill the evil spirit inside her. And that is when Aiyasha started to look worried.

With a frown on her face, she replied, 'If they kill me, what will become of little Elah here? How will the other orphans manage when they come back from school? Will they be allowed to complete their schooling?'

Olivia put her arm around Aiyasha. 'Don't worry,' she said. 'We won't let them kill you.'

'That's right,' said Audrey. 'We promise we will make a plan to get you out of this situation. We are friends now and we will do anything to support a friend in need.'

Audrey and Olivia said they needed to get back or Miss Gooday would come looking for them. But they promised to return the next day with a plan.

Chapter 4

A poison-prompted plan

On the long walk back to their tents, Olivia and Audrey came up with the idea of taking Aiyasha and me back with them to England and to their school. The general idea seemed pretty good. But, as they thought more about it, they identified a couple of difficulties.

First, to get from Bundami to England would entail travelling across lots of borders between countries. Aiyasha and I didn't have passports. But then the girls thought of hiding us in the overland truck while they went across these borders. There was a large space at the back of the luggage compartment where we could hide. This idea of treating Aiyasha and me as stowaways sounded really cool and exciting, and appealed to the girls' mischievous natures.

Olivia and Audrey were sure they could persuade the rest of the sixth form girls to cooperate with this plan. But what about Miss Gooday? They would have to work on Miss Gooday.

Then there was the issue of how to get permission for Aiyasha and me to stay in England and become pupils with them at Petranians College for Girls. Olivia thought there would be no problem with getting us two orphans accepted at the school and that her dad would definitely pay for us. Getting residence status for two orphans might be more difficult. But Olivia thought that this was where her dad could help. He had gone to the same school as the Prime Minister. He knew a school friend, who knew someone, who knew someone, who knew someone who had the private telephone number of the Prime Minister. Something could be arranged. Everyone knew that anything could be arranged, as long as you knew the right people.

The plan seemed watertight. It only remained to win over Miss Gooday. Surely, they thought, if they emphasised how much 'doing good' the rescue of two at-risk orphans would do, then Miss Gooday would be persuaded to go along with it.

That evening at the girls' camp, Olivia and Audrey were unusually helpful in preparing the meal, cooking it and clearing it away. Miss Gooday was surprised, but pleased these two were being so helpful for a change. It was when the two girls asked to have a private word with her that she thought there may have been more to this helpfulness than she first imagined.

Miss Gooday listened to the girls' account of their visit to the orphan hut, and how the community had accused Aiyasha of being a witch and the threat of poisoning. As she listened, her expression became more and more concerned. When they then explained their stowaway plan and the idea of the orphans becoming pupils at Petranians College, her brow began to furrow. She was obviously thinking of the problems involved.

When the girls had finished, Miss Gooday remained quiet for a moment.

'I think, like you, this is a terrible thing that has happened to the two orphans and I would like to help,' she said. 'I admire you for your concern and imagination, but you must realise that what you are proposing is against the law of this country and of our country.'

Nobody said anything for some minutes. All three of them sat there, thinking.

Then Miss Gooday spoke up. 'Tomorrow, you must take me to meet Aiyasha and Elah. We will go straight after we have finished breakfast.'

With that, she said goodnight and went to her tent.

* * *

The next morning, Miss Gooday, Olivia and Audrey drove to the orphan hut in the pickup truck she had hired for the project. When they got there, all was quiet. They tapped on the iron door. They heard faint groaning from inside the hut.

They pushed open the door to see Aiyasha and me lying on our sleeping mats, unable to move. Aiyasha pointed to a bowl of porridge that we had been eating from, but not cleaned.

She looked up at Miss Gooday and whispered, 'Poison.'

Miss Gooday was frozen with shock. She just stared at us lying on the floor and then slowly looked around the rest of the hut. Then she moved quickly.

'Help me put these poor girls in the back of the truck,' she said to Olivia and Audrey. 'We must take them to the clinic and quickly.'

There was a clinic just outside the city and Miss Gooday drove there as fast as she could. It was a very bumpy ride: first on narrow tracks, and then a stony gravel road. She pulled up outside the clinic in a cloud of dust and ran into the reception area, ahead of a waiting queue of mothers with babies on their backs.

Miss Gooday explained to the nurse that she had two young girls who had been poisoned and they needed to be treated with a stomach pump to remove as much of the poisoned food as possible. She told the nurse she must hurry or they would die.

The doctor and nurses on duty acted fast. They put tubes down our throats and sucked out the contents of our stomachs. It was quite painful and I kept feeling as if I was going to be sick. Afterwards, the doctor gave me an injection and I went to sleep.

When Miss Gooday, Olivia and Audrey came back to the clinic three hours later, Aiyasha and I were sitting up in beds next to each other. We were very weak, but we were going to live.

Miss Gooday sat between us and spoke, mostly to Aiyasha. 'Olivia and Audrey told me about your situation. They wanted to take you back with us to England. Last night, I thought it was too risky. However, your near death this morning has convinced me we must take the risk. It is the only way to save you. We are going to smuggle you back to England and give you new lives there.'

Aiyasha smiled a silent thank you, but then she looked worried. 'What about the orphans at school?' she said softly. 'We must let them know.'

Miss Gooday agreed to take Aiyasha to the school where the Bundu Bunch were studying so she could explain what had happened and how she and I were going to escape to safety.

That is how the most amazing adventure started for me. I had never been away from the Bundami valley. Now, I was going to travel across lands I could never have imagined. I can't remember it all. But I will tell you about the bits I do remember.

Chapter 5

Escape with a forbidden feast

The next day I was still feeling very weak. While I stayed in bed in the clinic, Aiyasha took Miss Gooday to the Bundu Bunch's school.

I don't know what they said or how the Bundu Bunch responded. What I do know is that they accepted that Aiyasha and I must escape in the overland truck. I also know they promised to write to us at Petranians College to let us know how they were doing at school and how they were treated in the community.

Two days later, my adventure started. Late that evening, everyone in the community was at the party arranged to say thank you and goodbye to the Petra girls. This was the one time Meyego brought the community together – for parties and celebrations, especially when someone else was contributing to or paying for the food.

While all were enjoying the food, music and dancing, Olivia and Audrey smuggled Aiyasha and me into the back of the overland truck. All we brought with us was a blanket each and Aiyasha's briefcase.

Much to our delight, Olivia and Audrey brought us some food from the party. We orphans are the only household that Meyego never invited to his community party feasts. We had heard about them and about how they usually included roasting a goat on a spit, rice and beans and buns and soda. It was the best meal I can remember having. And it was all the more enjoyable for knowing that we were saying goodbye to Meyego by participating in one of his forbidden feasts.

We settled down for the night in the back of the truck with our blankets over us. As we went to sleep, Aiyasha spoke softly to me.

'A new life is starting for us, Elah. But I will come home to Bundami one day.'

I was happy to be leaving the Bundami valley with people who seemed to care for us. And I was excited about what was to come.

* * *

The next morning, the girls packed up their tents, had a quick breakfast and we were off. We were told to keep our heads down until we had driven out of the valley. We drove through other valleys like ours and then, after a while, the truck stopped. Everyone got out and had a drink under a shady tree. When it was time to start again, Miss Gooday told Aiyasha and me that we were near the first border and she asked us to get into the storage compartment at the back of the truck. We took our blankets and settled down in the dark.

Before long, the truck stopped again. We heard people getting down from the truck and, after a little while, they came back again. The truck started up and moved slowly for a short time before stopping again. The same thing happened. People got out and then got back on. All the while, Aiyasha and I were keeping mousy quiet, as we had been told to do.

The truck moved off, faster this time. The next stop was under another tree. Olivia came to the luggage compartment to get a small table. She told us we could get out and join everyone else for a picnic lunch.

'Well done, guys,' she said. 'That was our first border crossing. You have left your country behind and you are safe from Mr Meyego.'

As I looked around this new country, it didn't seem much different from ours. The houses looked the same, the cattle looked the same, the people looked the same.

I said to Aiyasha, 'This country looks just like Bundami.'

'Yes, Elah,' replied Aiyasha, 'but in the days to come, you will see differences. I want you to notice the differences and we will talk about them. We will look at a map in my ABC book to identify the different countries we pass through. This trip will be a practical geography lesson for you and for me. We are very lucky to have this opportunity.'

'Typical Aiyasha,' I thought. 'She can never stop teaching. Now she no longer has the Bundu Bunch, she has started on me.'

My next thought was, 'I hope she won't be disappointed because I don't think she will find such a responsive learner in me compared with the Bundu Bunch.'

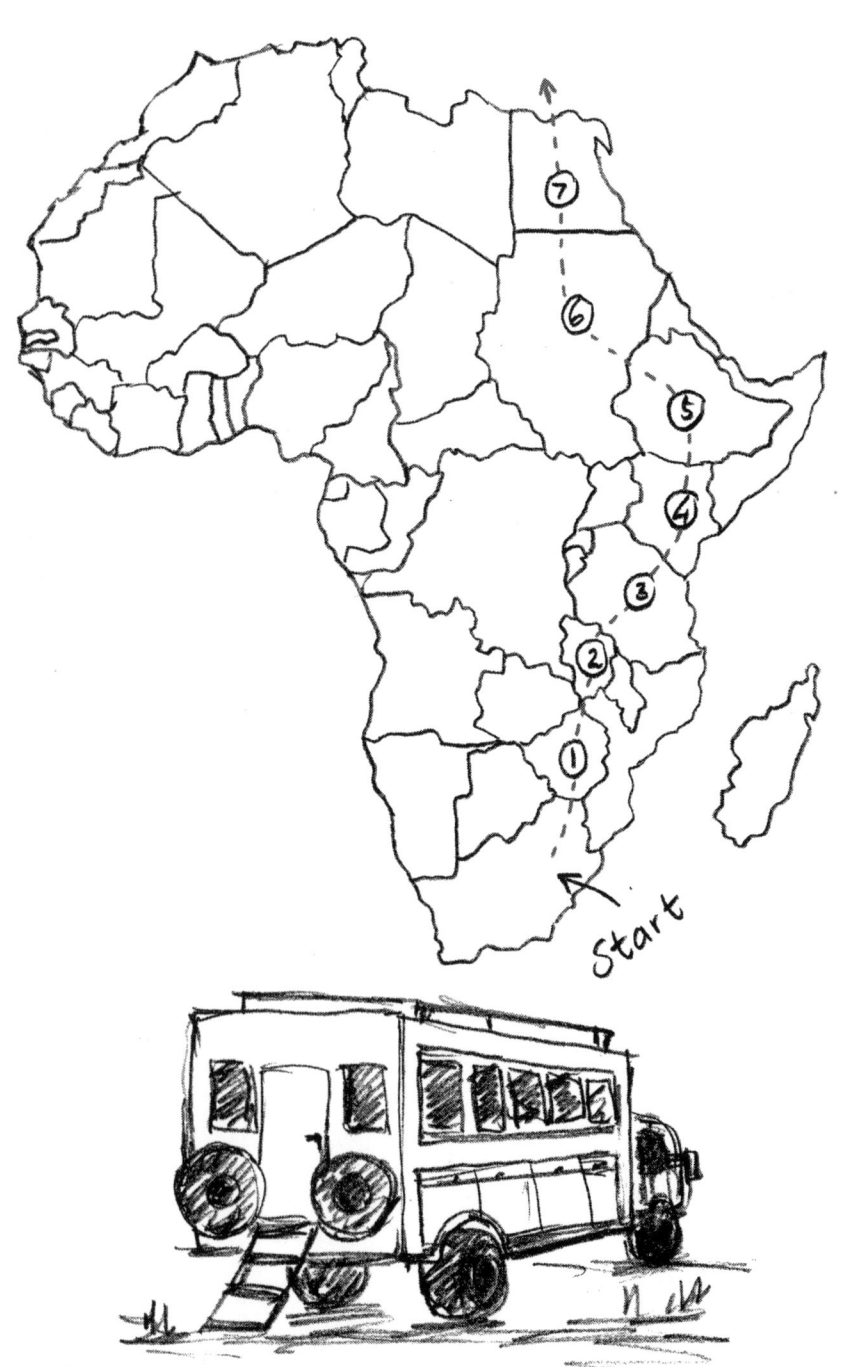

Chapter 6

Africa to Greece

I am not sure how much geography I learnt. After all, I was only five years old. But I do remember that we started at the bottom of the continent of Africa and we travelled through seven different countries to the very top.

I can tell you some things I remember about each of these countries, which I will identify by the order we visited them because, at the time, that's how I remember them. Maybe you can get a map and find the names of each country marked on the map Aiyasha took from her ABC book.

Country 1

Most of this country looked very much like home in the Bundami valley. I remember the trees were bigger. There was one tree that looked as though it had been planted upside down because its roots seemed to be reaching for the sky. These trees had enormous trunks and no leaves on their root-branches.

This is where we had a bit of an accident. Miss Gooday wanted to show the girls a man-made lake which was the biggest in the world when it was first created by building a huge dam wall across the Zambezi river. The driver took the truck off the road onto an open area leading to the lake. Suddenly, it lurched to one side and came to a jolting stop. One of the front wheels had sunk into a deep hole.

Miss Gooday asked everyone to get out while the driver tried to drive the truck out of the hole. He revved the engine loudly, but there was just a lot of dust and no movement. We were stuck, alone, in the middle of nowhere. Well, not quite alone. As we sat on the grass, we noticed a few huge elephants coming out of some trees, heading for the lake. Aiyasha pointed to them and got me to count: one, two, three, four, five … Soon, I could not keep up with the numbers. And anyway, I lost concentration as the girls excitedly pointed out baby elephants among the others.

The girls were taking pictures with their cameras.

'Look at that tiny one walking under its Mum!' they shouted.

'Look at that one with huge tusks!'

'Look at them drinking and spraying water with their trunks!'

While we watched the elephants drinking and washing themselves, other animals came to the lake

to drink. We saw buck of all sizes, some with huge screw-like horns, some with horns that were curved and very sharp-looking. We saw giraffe, rhino, ugly cattle called wildebeest, and black-and-white striped zebra.

We were all entranced by this magical spectacle of so many animals coming and going to the water and then disappearing again into the bush. Then we heard the sound of an engine. In the time we had been watching the animals, our driver had walked back to the road and managed to wave down another vehicle which had come to help pull our truck out of the hole.

By the time we were back on the road it was getting dark, and we still had a long drive to the hostel where Miss Gooday had planned for us to stay. In the dark, the truck headlights shone into the bush on either side of the road and we began to see eyes reflected back at us. Animals of the bush, Miss Gooday told us, have different-coloured eyes. The grazing animals who eat grass and leaves have green eyes. Animals who eat the meat of other animals have red eyes. We spent the rest of the drive scanning the bush with torches to look for green and red eyes. It kept me awake, just.

Countries 2 and 3

What I remember about these countries is that we camped at night in game parks. To get to these countries, though, we had to go across a very scary bridge. To reduce the weight of the truck, everyone had to get out and walk across the bridge. The bridge went over a narrow and very deep gorge, just below the most magnificent waterfall in the world. The waterfall in Bundami below which Sipho had taught me to swim seemed a trickle in comparison. As we walked across the bridge, our ears were filled with the roar of falling water and our clothes were soaked with spray. I held onto the railings very tightly and walked very carefully.

Oh, yes, I was going to tell you about my memories of camping in the game parks. This was exciting and, at the same time, a little scary.

One evening, we camped on a bank above a river. A few of the girls had gone down to the river for a walk. Miss Gooday told them to be careful and not go too near the bank, as there may be crocodiles lurking. After a while, we heard their shouts and screams. It was not a crocodile they were scared of. It was a hippo. They raced up the path from the river, shouting, 'Hippo, hippo!' as they ran towards us, looking over their shoulders.

Soon we saw a huge hippo behind them, and gaining on them. The girls got to the top of the bank and ran behind the truck. The hippo kept on coming. It ran right past the truck to the bush beyond and, as our eyes followed it, we saw the backside of a second hippo running away. Later on, the first hippo came slowly down the path, past the truck and launched itself gracefully back into the water. Our driver told us the first hippo had been chasing away the second hippo from its favourite spot on the river. The girls were not so keen on going for game park walks on their own after that.

That evening, we were sitting around a campfire. Beyond the fire, on the edge of the campsite clearing, we heard noises in the bush. When the girls shone their torches in that direction, we saw lots of pairs of eyes looking back at us. And these eyes were red. People in the camp told us they were hyaenas, waiting for scraps of our roasted supper.

The next morning, Aiyasha and I woke up to hear a bit of a commotion outside. The girls who were on breakfast cooking duty were going round the tents asking who knew where the saucepans and pots and kettle were. Nobody could give an answer. Then, one of the girls who was coming back from the toilet shouted out.

'I've found one here, in the bush.' Then she added, 'But the handle is gone. It's just the pan with no handle.'

The other pots and pans were found in the bushes nearby. All without handles.

Hyaenas have very strong jaws with which they can easily crack open bones of dead animals. These hyenas had liked the taste of what we had cooked in our pots and pans. Their jaws had been strong enough to eat the plastic handles, but not the iron parts of the pots. For the rest of the trip, the girls learnt to cook with pots without handles.

* * *

The scariest experience we had was on the last night in country 3. After supper and a bit of gossip round the campfire, the girls went to their tents to sleep, while Aiyasha and I went to sleep in the truck, as usual.

I awoke to see some girls climbing into the truck with their sleeping bags.

'What are you doing here?' Aiyasha asked them. 'It's the middle of the night.'

'Didn't you hear it?' one girl said. 'The lion roar was very close.'

Then we heard it. The roar was indeed very, very close and it was very, very loud. More girls climbed into the truck with their sleeping bags. They were scared of the lions and thought it would be safer to spend the night in the truck than in their tents.

The next morning, Olivia and Audrey were up first. Slowly they opened the truck door and looked

around the campsite. All was quiet. There were no lions, but they had left their visiting cards. These were in the form of huge paw prints which circled every tent and led away into the bush.

All the girls had abandoned their tents to sleep in the truck.

One of them said, 'Where's Miss Gooday?'

Another replied, 'She must be in her tent.'

Olivia plucked up courage to go to Miss Gooday's tent to look for her. 'Miss Gooday, Miss Gooday, are you OK?' she called.

There was no answer.

The girls went all around the campsite calling out for Miss Gooday.

Miss Gooday could not be found.

By now, the girls were very worried. 'What are we going to do without Miss Gooday?' they asked each other.

Everyone thought Miss Gooday must have been taken by the lions. Then the driver came over. He had been sleeping in his own tent some way away with the game park guards.

'What's the problem?' he asked. 'Why is everyone by the truck already?'

The driver said he did not think the lions would have taken Miss Gooday. He went to her tent and looked at the ground outside the entrance to look for signs of a body being dragged away. By this time, however, the girls had trampled all over the ground there and it was not possible to tell.

The driver was now beginning to look worried.

Then we heard a familiar voice from the edge of the campsite.

'Good morning, everyone. Is breakfast ready? I've been on a long, early morning walk and I'm famished and ready for my coffee.' It was Miss Gooday.

Miss Gooday was very surprised to get the greeting of her life from the girls. They all ran up to her and gave her a hug and told her how relieved they were to see her.

'Wow!' she exclaimed. 'I should go on an early morning walk more often.'

Country 4

On the way to the capital city of country 4, we marvelled at the magnificent sight of Africa's highest mountain rising up out of the parkland plain below. It had a white covering on its peak, like icing.

Aiyasha explained that the icing on the top was snow, which was freezing rain. I found it difficult to imagine freezing rain. It didn't sound very nice.

When we got there, the capital city gave me a shock. In some ways, it was an impressive shock. But it was also a horrible shock.

It was impressive to see so many people and cars and lorries. I didn't think it was possible for there to be so many in the whole world. I had never seen such large, high buildings before. The movement, noise and lights were bewildering. I remember thinking I must keep hold of Aiyasha or else I would get swallowed up and lost in this fascinating, frightening world.

I was in for an even greater shock as we wove our way through the city. At one point, the road went next to a railway line. On the other side of the railway line there was a different city. It was a city of Bundami orphan huts. But the huts were more badly built than ours. They not only had tin sheets for roofs, but they also had tin sheets for walls. And hundreds of huts were crammed next to each other, for as far as we could see.

The girls were as shocked as me. 'How can people live in these conditions?' they asked each other. I could see that Aiyasha was also taken aback. She stared and stared, but didn't say anything.

We were all happy to leave the capital city behind us, although the sights and sounds remained with us.

Countries 5, 6 and 7

The last three countries we passed through, before we boarded a ship to cross the sea, were very different from our Bundami valley.

What I noticed most was that they were very dry, very dusty and quite smelly. In the first country, it was so dry that there were no maize fields like we had in Bundami and had seen in all the other countries so far. Instead of maize porridge, the people ate what looked like a round piece of toilet paper in which they wrapped meat and vegetables. They called this *injera*. It is made from grass seeds and tastes quite sour.

In the other two countries, they grew crops using irrigated water from a huge river called the Nile. In one place, it was so hot and dusty that we didn't sleep in our tents but on the flat roof of a hostel so we could catch a little breeze and get away from the dust and smell below.

The thing that struck me most was that, in the villages we passed, many young boys were on crutches. They had parts of their legs missing. Aiyasha told me there had been a lot of fighting in the years before and armies had put explosive mines along the roads and tracks in the war zones.

Travelling through these countries made me realise how lucky I was to have lived in the Bundami valley, with no history of war and its lush green maize fields, cool bright air and maize porridge instead of sour toilet paper to eat.

Chapter 7

Greta's Grecian grudge

I was worried about the overland truck falling into the water as it was driven up the ramp to the ship that was to take us to Greece. But all was well and the driver managed to squeeze it on a deck between lots of other cars and lorries.

We were leaving Africa behind and heading for Greece, where we were going to camp for two nights before travelling through Italy to England.

After the truck drove off the ship, the driver took us on a winding road into the hills. The sea was always near and I longed to stop and get out and swim in the shining water. After a while, we drove down a narrow road to a grassy slope above a bay. This was where we were going to camp for two nights.

It had been a long and hot day of travelling and everyone was keen to get into the inviting water that lay just below us. The girls went down to the beach with their towels and carefully stepped into the sea. I went to a rock ledge and dived in. The water was crystal clear and warm and deep. You could dive down and down.

It felt wonderful and I swam under the water for as long as I could. When I surfaced, I noticed the girls some way away on the beach. They were all waving their hands and calling my name. I swam towards them, duck-diving on the way, enjoying the feeling of freedom, swimming like a dolphin through the water.

When I got to them, the girls clustered around me asking if I was OK. I assured them I was perfectly fine and feeling just great.

It turned out they were very worried when they saw me dive from the rock ledge. They never thought a 5-year-old could swim, let alone dive and survive in deep water.

I spent many hours during the next two days teaching some of the girls how to dive from ledges and how to swim and duck-dive from the surface. I felt very proud to be teaching these girls, who were so much older than me. I kept saying to myself, 'Thank you, Sipho, for teaching me how to swim in our pool under the waterfall.'

As we sat by our tents that evening, listening to the water lapping gently at the stones on the beach, it all seemed to be going 'swimmingly', you could say.

What I have come to learn is that you need to be wary when everything seems to be going 'swimmingly'. Usually, the glow of pleasure and satisfaction doesn't last long, and often there is something in the background getting ready to dim the outlook.

What I hadn't noticed was that one of the girls, called Greta, resented the fact I was teaching her and the other girls how to swim. One reason was that she was not any good at it. She was not prepared to put her head under the water because, she said, 'I don't want to get my hair messed up.'

But the truth of it was that she was scared. I tried to show her how she could overcome her fear, but she said, 'I don't need any help from you.'

Greta had taken herself off back to the tents while the rest of us continued our fun on and under the water. The girls lined up one behind the other and we had a competition to see how many sets of legs we could swim under. I managed six, but I didn't win.

The next day, Greta's resentment of me spread to Aiyasha because of the outcome of the training run that Miss Gooday set up after breakfast.

Miss Gooday called us all together. 'Before you all head for the beach and the water, I want to start our training for next term's long-distance running events. I have spoken to the local farmer and he has shown me a path that goes from here, through his olive grove, and up to an old cafe called the Sundowner Tavern, at the top of the hill.

'Try to keep up with Greta, who will win, as she always does. There will be water for you at the top and you can have a three-minute rest there before you jog back down the hill.

'Remember, this is a training exercise to help you get into shape to cope with the races coming up next term. You will get the most benefit if you keep going as fast as you can, however tired you feel. No pain no gain.'

The girls went to their tents grumbling that they had come to Greece to sunbathe and swim, not for long-distance runs up hills.

'We do enough of that at Petra,' one of them said loudly.

Once all the girls were ready in their running kits, Miss Gooday set them off and Greta raced to the front to lead the way.

As Miss Gooday was about to get into the truck to drive to the Sundowner Tavern, Aiyasha put her hand up.

'Miss Gooday, please can I join in the run?' she asked.

Miss Gooday looked surprised for a moment. 'But they are well away by now,' she replied, 'and anyway, you don't have any running shoes.'

'Please, can I go, Miss Gooday?' said Aiyasha. 'I will catch them up.'

Miss Gooday found Aiyasha a spare pair of running shoes, some shorts and a top, and off she started after the others. Miss Gooday glanced at her watch before she climbed into the truck.

Left on my own, I went for a swim. Later, Audrey and Olivia told me what had happened during the run and why Greta was now saying unkind things about both Aiyasha and me.

Audrey was towards the back of the runners, after a while, she saw Aiyasha sail past them with an easy stride.

'Aiyasha was running as if the hill wasn't there,' said Audrey.

Soon, Aiyasha had overtaken Olivia as well. Audrey and Olivia said the climb was very steep and the hill seemed to go on and on. Greta was way out in front as usual. It was on the final bend round the mountain, with the Sundowner Tavern in sight, that Aiyasha drew level with Greta. She was very surprised to see Aiyasha and, not wanting to be beaten, she increased her pace. Aiyasha matched her, stride for stride. With a hundred metres to go, Aiyasha smoothly stretched her legs a little more and got to the tavern well ahead of Greta. Greta collapsed on the steps of the veranda of the tavern, gasping for breath. Aiyasha went to help her up and offered her a cup of water.

Greta looked up with a glower on her face. She knocked away the cup of water and, as she pulled herself up with the help of the railings, she said, 'I don't need help from a foreigner. I can manage perfectly well by myself, thank you.'

That was the second 'foreigner' whose offer of help had been rejected. Pride can be a positive strength, but it can also be poisonous when it is hurt.

Chapter 8

A letter from the Bundu Bunch

The overland truck drove through the gates of Petranians College for Girls and stopped in front of a large, impressive building, with two stories of huge windows running parallel to each other. There were many cars in the square in front of the building with older people standing next to them.

As each girl got out of the truck, she ran up to one of the cars and threw her arms around her waiting parents. There was shouting of names and lots of chatter. Aiyasha and I sat in the back of the truck. We didn't have any parents to run up to.

Nevertheless, we got a surprise greeting that, for us, was just as good. Miss Gooday came into the truck waving an envelope. It was a letter from the Bundu Bunch.

Bundami Valley

Dear Aiyasha and Elah,

We all felt so sad after Aiyasha came to tell us you were going to escape with the playground girls.

But we understood it was the only way for you to stay safe. We have got used to the idea now and we think the 'witch accusation' cloud could have a silver lining. If you can both attend the Petra school, it may open up opportunities for you that you could never have had if you had stayed in Bundami.

Despite the thought of you being so far away and not being able to see you in the holidays, we are all enjoying school and learning so many new things. We missed you terribly two weeks ago, when we went back to the orphan hut for the August holiday. The hut seemed so quiet and abandoned. But nothing had been disturbed. Nobody from the community had wanted to go near the hut because of its association with 'Aiyasha, the witch'.

We soon found out that there were some visitors who didn't care about witches and had taken up residence in your absence. Two spiders had woven webs in one corner. Hornets were making a nest under the outside roofing. We gave Jacob the job of relocating the spiders and removing the hornets' nest.

For the next visitor removal task, we had to call on Pele.

We were putting our mats and clothes bags in their usual places around the walls of the hut, when Sakhile shouted, 'Jacob, come quick.'

As Jacob came over, Sakhile said, 'There is a long, thin snake in the corner there. What do you think it is? Is it dangerous?'

Jacob took one look and shouted, 'Everyone out! Get well away from the door.'

Jacob then came out backwards and quietly closed the door behind him. He turned to us and said, 'The snake in there is a Black Mamba. In a single bite he has enough venom to kill all of us.'

Jacob explained that trying to shoo the snake out of the hut would be too dangerous. And that, even if we could get it out of the hut, it was likely that it would try to come back to where it had found a place to its liking.

We needed Pele. But where was he? When we arrived at the hut, Pele was very excited to be back and ran around it twice before disappearing into the long grass. Jacob called and called for him, but Pele did not appear.

Jacob said nobody should go into the hut while we waited for Pele to appear. So we waited. And waited. The sun went down below the mountain and the light faded. Jacob said we would have to sleep outside the hut as Pele could not attack the Black Mamba in the dark.

There was a bright moon and, before long, Pele appeared with a baby rock rabbit in his mouth. It was OK for him. His supper was sorted. But we had to go without as the bread and peanut butter we had brought with us was in Sakhile's bag, which was inside the hut. We preferred to starve, which we were quite used to, than to get bitten by a deadly snake, which we weren't.

Once it got light, Jacob opened the door and pushed Pele through, saying, 'Go, Pele, and get your breakfast.' Soon, Pele was in his strike mode. We watched through a crack in the wall as Pele circled the Mamba and darted in to deliver a bite and then darted out again as the Mamba tried to bite him. After about fifteen minutes, the Mamba started to get tired and moved slower and slower. Then Pele scored his goal with a lightning strike that bit the Mamba behind his head and cut his spine. The Mamba dropped his head to the floor and Pele finished him off. He dragged the Mamba behind him as he looked for a shady spot under a tree to enjoy his breakfast.

We enjoyed our bread and peanut butter breakfast as well as any we had ever had, and probably even better than Pele enjoyed his Mamba.

What we learnt from this is that, whenever we come back for holidays, the first thing we must do is put Pele into the hut to clear it of unwanted visitors.

Once we had settled into the hut safely, we had a fun holiday time in Bundami. But we missed having Elah with us on our trips to the bush and swimming with us in the pool under the waterfall.

We will write again soon.

Love from the Bundu Bunch.

After reading the letter to me, Aiyasha folded it up and put it in her briefcase. She smiled at me.

'They are doing OK,' she said. 'Just as I knew they would. They will make me proud.'

I returned her smile. But the smile I forced from my lips was not reflected in my eyes. 'Of course they will make you proud,' I said. 'They are the Bundu Bunch.'

I looked away thinking, 'I wish I could also make you proud, but I don't think I will ever be able to make you as proud of me as you are of them.'

Chapter 9

Poisonous pride

Miss Gooday went home for a rest. She was exhausted after having been responsible for the sixth-form girls for six weeks. She was relieved to have delivered them all safely back to their parents. She still felt responsible for Aiyasha and me, though. She introduced us to Matron Barbara and asked her to look after us in the school sanatorium until term started the following week.

On returning to Petra three days later to get ready for the start of term, Miss Gooday was told to go to the headmistress' office. With the headmistress was the Chairman of the school's Board of Governors.

Lord McHaughty was a large and imposing man. He spoke at people, not to them, and he was disinclined to listen. Apart from being the Chairman of the Board of Governors, he was Greta's dad.

As soon as Miss Gooday had closed the door behind her, without any greeting, Lord McHaughty began to speak.

'Miss Gooday,' he said, slowly and deliberately, 'I understand you have taken it upon yourself to unlawfully bring into this country, and to our school, two African girl orphans. What do you propose to do with these girls?'

Miss Gooday looked at the headmistress to see if she was going to be invited to sit on the chair in front of her desk. The headmistress nodded and Miss Gooday sat down slowly.

Then she looked up at Lord McHaughty, who was standing at the side of the headmistress' desk.

'Yes, Lord McHaughty. I brought these girls here for their safety. The older one, Aiyasha, survived an attempt on her life by the community where she lived, and the younger one is dependent on her. I intend to make an asylum application for their right to remain in the country, and I hope that, in time, they may obtain British citizenship. I will apply to the governors for scholarships, so the girls can be cared for and get a good education here at our school'

'Miss Gooday,' boomed Lord McHaughty, as he banged one hand on the desk and said the next few words firmly and loudly and deliberately. 'YOU … WILL … DO … NO … SUCH … THING. These girls are illegal immigrants. By law, they must go to an immigrant detention centre. The school will have nothing to do with them.'

'I am sorry you feel like that, Lord McHaughty,' responded Miss Gooday. 'I believe, if you met them and heard their full story, you might think differently.'

'I have no intention of spending my time on a meeting with these African orphans from a backward ex-colony,' said Lord McHaughty gruffly. 'My daughter has told me all about them and how they humiliated her on the trip. I have no sympathy for anyone who upsets my daughter and reduces her to tears. I will not stand for it.

'There is a Board of Governors' meeting in two weeks' time. The matter will be addressed then, and the formal and final decision on their transfer to the government immigrant detention centre will be communicated to you thereafter.'

Miss Gooday was not going to let the matter go so easily.

Bravely, she responded. 'Lord McHaughty, I am ashamed that a leader of our developed nation has as little regard for human rights as leaders of communities in "backward ex-colonies", as you call them. The poison of your daughter's pride will condemn these girls to a life with little or no prospects, just as surely as the poison of an outdated custom in a developing country.'

The headmistress quickly brought the meeting to an end. 'Thank you, Miss Gooday. I will speak to you later about your continued employment at this school. You may leave us now.'

Miss Gooday waited around the corner of the corridor until Lord McHaughty had stormed out. She then knocked on the headmistress' door.

'I think,' said Miss Gooday, as she walked in, 'this school will regret sending Aiyasha and Elah away. Apart from the humanitarian issue, Aiyasha is an exceptionally talented runner. I have never seen anything like it. Greta is good and she holds the records for all the school cross-country circuits. But in Greece, Aiyasha started minutes after Greta and still beat her easily, without pushing herself. I believe we have here the best schoolgirl runner in the country. Aiyasha could win next week's schools cross-country championships for us.

'As you know, we have not won any school championship competition for many years and our trophy shelf in the dining room remains empty. If we play this right, we might not only improve the school's sporting reputation, but it could also be very good for our public relations when it is discovered that Petranians supports disadvantaged girls from developing countries.

'I have a friend who is the sports journalist on the *Newcastle Echo* newspaper. If the result of the championships next week is as I expect, then I think we may be able to get Lord McHaughty to change his mind and accept that his daughter will have to swallow her pride.'

The headmistress listened patiently. 'Well,' she replied, 'the Governors' meeting is not until the week after the championships. We will have Aiyasha and Elah with us until after that, at least. If what you say is correct, you may do as you plan. But, if it doesn't work out and Lord McHaughty does not change his mind, then we will have no alternative but to send Aiyasha and Elah to the detention centre.'

Chapter 10

Petranians College for Girls

Petranians College for Girls is a boarding school, which was established ages ago to educate the daughters of the landed gentry from the north of England. The school was organised into six houses, one of which was the junior school.

The houses were named after famous historical British ladies. In the senior school they were: Nightingale, Franklin, Lovelace, Pankhurst and Astor. The matron told Aiyasha she would be in Franklin house. I was to be allocated to Potter, the house in the junior school.

Each house had a long dormitory with forty beds arranged in two rows opposite each other. The most senior girls were at the top end, near the bathrooms. The most junior girls were at the bottom end. The dormitories were on the upper floors. Below each dormitory was a house common room, where the girls spent time when they were not at lessons, on the sports field or in the chapel. We didn't get to spend much time in our common rooms.

The dining room was a huge hall. Each house had a long table. The most senior girls sat at the top end of the table, the most junior ones sat at the bottom. On the wall, at the end of each house table, were flags. Each house had its own flag. But some had others, as well. I was told that these other flags meant that the house was the current champion for sports activities, such as netball, lacrosse and tennis. It struck me that flags were very important things in this school.

Each meal started with a grace, said by a prefect from the top table, where all the teachers sat. The school flag was on the wall by the top table. Under it was a shelf, with nothing on it. Rules seemed to be as important as flags at this school. Only after the teachers started to eat could anyone else begin. And only after the girl higher up on your table started, could you begin your meal.

It was all quite intimidating to start with. But I didn't care what funny rituals and customs I had to follow. I was getting three good meals a day for the first time in my life and I soon got into the swing of things.

Aiyasha was in the same house as Olivia and Audrey. I didn't see much of her, as my house, Potter, was in a separate building from the senior school. However, I did get to see her from a distance once every day as we went into and out of chapel, and three times on Sundays. Also, on Sundays after chapel, we had time to ourselves to go where we wanted and we always met up then.

I did feel a bit lonely at first. Most of the girls were nice, but they talked a lot about things I didn't know anything about. Like ponies, pantomimes, plays, pizza, pancakes, pianos, pigtails, polo, paddle boards, parties, parks, podcasts and playlists, as well as many other things that did not start with 'P'. So, they didn't take much interest in me. That all changed after the cross-country championships.

Chapter 11

Lord McHaughty's conversion

Miss Gooday had three days to prepare her team for the national schools cross-country championships. Each school was allowed to enter three runners. Aiyasha, Greta and Olivia were selected for the Petra team. At first, Greta was still angry with Aiyasha. But Aiyasha had learnt how to handle people who were antagonistic towards her.

Aiyasha started by talking about the team and how privileged she felt to be part of it. She said she had never been included in a sports team before. She talked about the strength of the team being greater than the individuals in it. She talked about how nobody had taught her anything about training, running or race strategy before, and how she was learning so much from Greta and Olivia.

Slowly, Greta's attitude to Aiyasha began to thaw. When Miss Gooday began talking with the team about their opponents and how to compete against them, Greta started to accept Aiyasha as a team member who would help them win. The school that had won the championships in the previous two years, and was favourite to win again, was Amplestone College.

Last year's champion runner was still at Amplestone College, and she was the favourite to win the individual championship. However, the team result depended on the placement of the first two runners. A school had to get one of their runners into the first eight places to score any points. The scoring went like this: 1st place = 10 points, 2nd = 8, 3rd = 6, 4th = 5, 5th = 4, 6th = 3, 7th = 2, 8th = 1.

A school with runners in first and ninth places would get 10 points. But a school with runners in third and fourth places would beat them with 11 points.

This meant that you didn't need a runner in your team to win the race in order to win the team trophy. If you could get two of your team members ahead of the second-placed runner in another team by more than one place, you would beat them. This was the thinking on which Miss Gooday based her race strategy.

The plan went like this. Olivia was to start really fast. But she wouldn't get too far ahead to make sure the other runners tried to keep up with her fast start. Greta and Aiyasha were to hang back, maintaining a steady pace for the first half of the course. As the runners ahead slowed down after their too-fast start, Greta and Aiyasha would increase their pace and overtake them. In this way, Greta and Aiyasha would finish ahead of most of the runners, including the second runner in the Amplestone team.

The day of the race arrived. A large crowd was gathered at the start/end point. There were parents, teachers, governors, and pupils. There were also some journalists, including Miss Gooday's friend from the *Newcastle Echo*.

The runners were checked off on the entry form, the rules were explained and the starting gun was fired. Off they all went, with Olivia in the lead. All the schools were cheering their runners. The Petra pupils cheered loudly when they saw one of their runners at the front.

Olivia did her job extremely well and stretched the runners out as they tried to keep up with her. All was going as planned at the halfway mark. But the second half of the race didn't turn out quite as Miss Gooday expected.

Just after the halfway mark, Greta and Aiyasha passed Olivia, who told them she had been passed by two Amplestone girls. Greta and Aiyasha passed a few more girls, but none were Amplestonians. At the last marker before the turn for the final pull up the hill to the finish, they were told they were in third and fourth places. They saw one Amplestonian ahead. They gradually gained on her and managed to overtake. Now they were in second and third places.

But that was still not enough with Amplestone being in first and fourth places. One of them had to catch up and go past the race leader.

They saw the leader and gave chase together.

After a while, Greta looked across at Aiyasha running beside her. 'Aiyasha, you go on your own. I'm holding you back.'

So Aiyasha accelerated up to the shoulder of the leader. As Aiyasha went past, the leader stuck out one leg and tripped her up. Aiyasha went sprawling on the ground. She was getting up again as Greta went past her.

'I'll get her for that,' said Greta. Greta was so furious about what she had seen, it gave her an extra boost of energy and she went into the lead on the last bend before the finish line.

Petranians first and third places. Amplestonians second and fourth.

They had won. They had done it together as a team. Greta ran over to Aiyasha and threw her arms about her. The two girls held each other tight, united and reconciled in victory. Greta had tears pouring down her cheeks.

The Petra girls watching at the finish went wild.

'We are the champions, we are the champions,' they chanted.

'Greta is our champion.'

'Petra are the champions.'

'Greta, Petra. Greta, Petra, Greta, Petra, Greta Pet…'

Miss Gooday allowed herself a half smile. Her smile was lit by the joy of success, but constrained by the hope for more.

She went up to Lord McHaughty. 'Lord McHaughty, may I introduce you to the sports journalist from the *Newcastle Echo*.'

'Pleased to meet you,' said the journalist to Lord McHaughty. 'Congratulations on a great win for Petranians. I would like to do a short interview with you about your wonderful girl champions.' They shook hands briefly. 'Please can I take a picture of you with them?'

Lord McHaughty liked nothing better than to be the centre of attention, and it couldn't get better than having his picture in the newspapers.

Greta, Aiyasha and Olivia were asked to come and stand next to Lord McHaughty, while the journalist took lots of pictures from many different angles.

The journalist then took out his notebook and started his interview. 'Lord McHaughty, congratulations on a great win for your school. And, I believe further congratulations are due to you and your school governors for your new scholarship programme for disadvantaged girls from developing countries.

'Our readers would be most interested to hear about this, especially as one of them has contributed to your success today.'

'What? Er, hum, oh yes, yes,' said Lord McHaughty.

The next day, the front page of the *Newcastle Echo* had a picture of a beaming Lord McHaughty next to Greta and Aiyasha, with Greta holding the national schools cross-country trophy. The headline read:

Petranians' enlightened scholarship programme strikes gold and topples ex-champions Amplestone against all expectations.

The article that followed talked a little bit about the race and a lot about how enlightened Lord McHaughty was to have established the Petranians' scholarship for disadvantaged girls from developing countries.

The following week, the headmistress received the minutes of the meeting of the Board of Governors, in which the scholarship programme was formally approved and the first two recipients were confirmed. They were, of course, Aiyasha and me.

When Miss Gooday saw a copy of the minutes, her face beamed with a full and unconstrained smile.

Chapter 12

Fast-track

In the following year, Aiyasha and I settled into a busy school routine at Petra, with wonderful holidays spent with the families of Olivia, Audrey and Greta. Olivia and Audrey lived near to each other and, when we stayed at either house, we always did things together. I especially enjoyed the days we spent on our bikes, exploring the countryside. We cycled to lakes where we fished and swam and built a raft out of fallen logs. We biked up mountain paths and had picnics at the top before hurtling back down. We discovered woods with patches of ripe raspberries and greengage trees. We tasted apples and pears from branches overhanging into narrow lanes.

Staying with Greta at McHaughty Manor was a bit more formal. There were strict meal times, to which we had to conform. Our free time revolved around the ponies and horses. We learnt to ride and to jump over fences. We joined hunts on horseback. We went to gymkhanas and horse trials, where we slept in a horsebox. We also spent a lot of time looking after the horses: mucking out, cleaning saddles and stirrups, and grooming.

Aiyasha and Greta had become great friends and training partners. Miss Gooday had spotted Aiyasha's special talent for distance running in that first training run in Greece. She knew that, with proper training, Aiyasha could become a champion.

Miss Gooday contacted the athletics coach for the North East of England, who was called Mo Grindley. She developed a grinding training routine for Aiyasha and Greta. Training with Aiyasha was good for Greta. Her competitive spirit compelled her to keep up with Aiyasha and she pushed herself hard to do so. Greta knew she could never match Aiyasha's talent, but that was no longer a concern for her. Ever since the cross-country race, where she conceded that she was holding Aiyasha back, her feelings for Aiyasha had turned from resentment to admiration.

The two girls began to win middle- and long-distance events. First at national school level, then at regional level, and then at full national level.

At the national athletics championship in Gateshead, Aiyasha and Greta were entered for the 1,000 metres, the 3,000 metres steeplechase and the 5,000 metres. In the 1,000 metres, Aiyasha won and Greta came third. The result was the same in the 3,000 metres steeplechase. In the 5,000 metres, Greta came in first, just ahead of Aiyasha, who eased up in the last 50 metres.

At the next training session, Mo Grindley excitedly waved a piece of paper at Miss Gooday. 'Great news! Greta has been selected to run for England at the Commonwealth Games next summer.'

'That's wonderful,' said Miss Gooday. 'But what about Aiyasha?'

Mo Grindley explained that Aiyasha was not a British national, so she could not represent England.

* * *

Greta and Aiyasha were both awarded places at Newcastle University the year before the Commonwealth Games. They continued to train together at Newcastle, but at weekends Greta joined the England squad and Aiyasha trained on her own.

Greta missed her training partner when she was with the England squad and her performances started to deteriorate. Her father, Lord McHaughty, eventually asked her why her times were not improving, despite training with the England squad.

'Dad,' she replied, 'I just don't enjoy the training any more, knowing that Aiyasha cannot aim for the England team with me.'

Lord McHaughty checked his list of private contacts and made a call the next day, which went like this.

Lord McHaughty: 'Hello, Prime Minister. It's Jacob here. Jacob McHaughty. How are you liking the flat? So glad I could help there. I wonder if you could do me a favour?'

PM: 'What ho! Nice to hear from you, McHaughty. What can I help you with?'

Lord McHaughty: 'There's a gal from our school who is a gold medal prospect in the Commonwealth Games next year. She has been stymied by your Home Office asylum seeker process and is not eligible to be considered for British nationality for two more years. Therefore, she cannot represent England in the games.

I am sure your Home Office Minister is *pretty* capable of bullying her staff into making an exception in this case and fast-tracking the approval. After all she owes you one, if you get my meaning.'

PM: 'Shouldn't be a problem, old boy. Leave it with me. All for the benefit of Queen and Country. Fast-track it will be.'

And fast-track it was. The following week, Mo Grindley got a letter from Athletics England saying she could include Aiyasha in the England training squad.

Chapter 13

The Bundu Bunch Bombshell

I did warn you to watch out when things all seem to be going swimmingly.

Everything was turning out so well. Aiyasha and Greta were at Newcastle University training together. They were in the England squad for the Commonwealth Games to be held in three months' time. Aiyasha's coaches were confident she would do well and could even win a gold medal.

I was looking forward to moving up to Petra 8–12 prep school with my friends next year.

I was in the Potter house common room when I looked up from the chessboard and saw Aiyasha standing in front of me.

'What are you doing here?' I asked. 'Why are you not at university?'

From the look on her face, I knew she was not happy about something. I soon discovered what.

Aiyasha showed me the letter from the Bundu Bunch. 'There is bad news from Bundami.'

She explained the situation to me.

The agency sponsoring scholarships in Africa had had their budget cut by their government as part of a policy to reduce overseas aid spending. The schools had not been paid for the coming term. The orphan cousins were told they could no longer attend school and must go back home. When they got back to the orphan hut, Meyego was waiting for them. Meyego told them he wanted to rent the land the hut was on to a man from the city and they must therefore take their things and leave Bundami.

Monica later found out that Meyego was renting plots of land in Bundami to people from the city. He was doing this to earn money to keep his son, Samu, at school now that the fees were no longer being paid by his scholarship.

The letter ended by telling us not to worry, that the Bundu Bunch were discussing their options and would make a plan to resolve the situation.

Of course, Aiyasha could not 'not worry'.

'I have come to tell you that I am going to ask Lord McHaughty to give me a loan,' said Aiyasha. 'I will then buy a plane ticket and go to Bundami to help the orphan cousins.'

'What are you going to do when you get there?' I asked.

'I don't know yet, but I will think of something,' she replied in a tired, quiet voice.

Now I was worried. Worried about the orphan cousins, and worried about Aiyasha.

'Aiyasha,' I said, 'you are not thinking clearly. By going to Bundami now, you will be giving up on your big chance to win a medal at the Commonwealth Games. You will be letting down those who have done so much to help you get this rare opportunity. You will be letting down Greta, Lord McHaughty, Mo Grindley and Miss Gooday.'

Aiyasha remained silent. I could see she was deep in thought.

I continued, 'I think your ideas are being affected by your feelings of guilt for leaving the Bundu Bunch alone in Bundami. I really do not think that the Bundu Bunch would want you to sacrifice everything you have achieved over the past few years, just to be with them.'

I told her there must be another way.

Through our shared adventure over the last years, I had grown close to Aiyasha and had come to gain some understanding of what was important to her and how she thought and felt. She was an achiever and thrived on a challenge. The achievements she sought were not for herself, but for the sake of others. I needed to remind her of what she might be giving up and who might gain or lose.

Aiyasha looked at me in surprise. 'Elah,' she said, 'that's the first time you have given me advice, and I think you may be right. Thank you for saying that. I am lucky to have you thinking more clearly than me. We do need to think out the options more carefully.'

Despite the situation, I was so pleased that Aiyasha was prepared to listen to me and that I could be of benefit to her. In fact, I was elated, though I knew that was a bit selfish given the circumstances.

* * *

Two days later, we got another letter from the Bundu Bunch. Thankfully, they had been thinking rationally and were working on a plan to stay on at the orphan hut. The letter had been written by Sipho.

Monica had visited a lawyer in Bundami to ask whether Meyego had the right to make them leave and rent the land to someone from the city. Monica was told that, according to the local law, the orphans were members of the community and had a right to live on community land.

However, the lawyer also told Monica that Meyego could rent out the land where the hut was and give the orphans another place to live. But Meyego could not force them to leave the hut if they could pay the rent he had agreed with the city man.

The Bundu Bunch decided to earn the money needed to pay the rent and to buy food for themselves. Langa and Luke were already doing repair work for people nearby. They had repaired radios and bicycles and were working on an old truck that had not been driven for a whole year.

Monica was collecting and selling herbs and wild spinach and had started a beehive to make honey to sell. Jacob had been hired to take Pele to some houses where the owners had been having problems with snakes attacking their chickens.

Jabu was working as a housemaid for a family who had just built a large house on land that Meyego had sold to them for a lot of money. Sipho was working as a gardener for them.

It was only Sakhile who did not have a paying job. She stayed at the hut and cleaned the yard and cooked for everyone. At school, she had learnt about solar power and was experimenting with different ways of using solar panels to do things such as heating the water and making lamps.

In this way, the Bundu Bunch had been getting enough money to pay Meyego his rent and to feed themselves.

* * *

Aiyasha was very proud of the orphan cousins when she heard of the initiatives they were taking to continue living in the orphan hut. However, she was concerned that their education had come to an end even before they'd finished primary school. She knew that, without getting an educational qualification, they would struggle to find good jobs. And she fretted that they were not getting the opportunity to have the bright futures she had envisaged for them when she left.

'Elah,' she said to me, looking very dejected, 'I can't believe that it is the donor who is responsible for my worst fears being realised. I imagined Meyego may somehow stop the Bundu Bunch completing their education so that he could go on calling them dumb orphans. I never thought that the donor would destroy the promise of fulfilling our dreams that they themselves had made seem possible.'

The next day, Mo Grindley came to see me at Petra to ask if I knew the reason why Aiyasha seemed to lack concentration and motivation in her training sessions. I told her that Aiyasha was worried about the orphan cousins back in Bundami.

Mo Grindley looked at me sternly and said, 'Whatever the reason, if Aiyasha goes on like this, she is unlikely to do well enough in the trials to get onto the England team, let alone win the gold medal of which she is capable.'

It seemed like the dreams we'd had a few days ago were an illusion. The dreams I had for Aiyasha, the dreams Aiyasha had for herself and for the Bundu Bunch, were evaporating.

But I hadn't factored in the tech-savvy genius of Olivia and Audrey.

Chapter 14

Dream on

It was Greta who first made Olivia and Audrey aware of Aiyasha's problem. Although they were now all at different universities, they met up regularly as a Skype group. After the Skype meeting when Greta explained why Aiyasha was no longer training properly, Olivia and Audrey agreed to meet up at home the following weekend.

When they met, Olivia wasted no time in formulating a plan of action. 'We need to be able to tell Aiyasha that the orphan cousins will be able to complete their schooling. Then she will get her motivation back and have a chance of going to the Commonwealth Games.'

'Yes, I agree,' said Audrey. 'But we can't just tell her the school fees will be covered. We have to convince her that we can come up with enough money to see them through the rest of primary school and the whole of high school.'

'I guess,' replied Olivia, 'but do you have any idea how much we are talking about? I have done some calculations and reckon this would cost about fifty-five thousand pounds.' She frowned for a moment. 'How many of your friends at Uni might make a contribution?'

'Well, let's see,' said Audrey. 'There are six on my course I get on well with. Then there's another eight in the netball team, and the four friends I hang out with in my hall of residence. That's what? Eighteen.'

Olivia did some calculating out loud.

'OK, about the same for me,' she said. 'Let's say we could find forty contributors from Uni. How much would they be prepared to give? Maybe twenty pounds each max? That would get us just eight hundred pounds. We need sixty times that amount.'

She thought for a moment. 'Let's look at it another way. To raise fifty-five thousand pounds, we need ten-pound contributions from five-and-a-half-thousand people. The only way we can do that is through social media.'

That is what led them to set up a fundraising campaign using the JustGiving crowdfunding platform.

They spent the weekend developing a funding appeal, with a target of £55,000. While they had been skiving off work when the group was building the playground in Bundami, they had wandered round the valley taking lots of photos. They had photos of the community, of the orphan hut, of the Bundu Bunch and of Aiyasha. They needed to put these photos together with a story about Aiyasha and the Bundu Bunch that was meaningful to the British public. It had to be topical, enlightening and to pull at heartstrings.

The heartstrings bit was not too difficult. There was the orphan hut, the lack of schooling, Aiyasha's classroom in the forest. The enlightening bit was covered in the story of Aiyasha's escape and adoption by Petranians College for Girls. But what about topical? It needed to be related to something in the forefront of people's minds right now. The implication of the government's reduction in its overseas aid budget on the scholarships was a bit topical. But they needed something more immediate and more meaningful to everyone.

Olivia and Audrey made a YouTube video with their photos about the Bundami story to go with their appeal. They posted the appeal on JustGiving and returned to their universities on Sunday evening. They told all their friends about the appeal and asked them to copy it to their friends. By the end of the week, the appeal fund had reached £200.

This was an encouraging start and good enough for them to decide to take the next move, which was to get Aiyasha motivated and focused on her training.

Olivia and Audrey travelled to Newcastle the next weekend to meet with her and Greta.

* * *

After the training session finished, the four of them gathered in Greta's room with takeaway pizzas. They sat on the bed, on the chair and on the floor.

'How did the training session go this afternoon?' asked Olivia.

'OK,' said Aiyasha without a smile. Greta looked down to the floor.

'Hey, guys,' said Audrey. 'Buck up. We know how to get the money we need to replace the scholarships for the Bundu Bunch. We've come here to tell you about it and what we need to do to make it work.'

Olivia and Audrey typed in the web address of their JustGiving appeal and got the campaign page up on their computer screen:

JustGiving

Aiyasha's Back us Orphans Campaign

Aiyasha is an orphan herself. She is hoping to be able to thank you for your support by winning a medal for England at the Commonwealth Games.

> **Story**
>
> The Government's overseas aid budget cuts have let down orphans around the world. Aiyasha is determined not to let down the seven orphans in her care. She is asking for your help to replace the promised scholarships that have been taken away by the aid cuts.
>
> *Play the YouTube video*
> *to meet Aiyasha and her orphans.*

Audrey let them read the appeal pitch before continuing.

'The website has been up for five days now and the campaign fund stands at just over £200,' she said. 'Contributions have come from family and friends and people who know you, Aiyasha. This will increase as friends tell their friends about you. But we need over 5,000 people to know about you to reach our target.'

'Gosh,' said Greta. 'How do we contact over 5,000 people?'

'We don't,' said Olivia. 'The newspapers and news websites will do that when you get into the England team for the Commonwealth Games.'

'Yes,' added Audrey, 'especially if you can run well at the final England trials in two weeks' time and achieve times as good as, or better than, the Kenyan favourites.'

Aiyasha's face slowly relaxed. Her eyes became wider and brighter. Her serious and determined look was back again. Her motivation was back.

She looked at her friends and said very slowly and determinedly, 'Thank you. I WILL DO IT.'

And she did.

* * *

Aiyasha came first in the England pre-games trials in the 5,000 metres and in the 10,000 metres. And her winning times were less than three seconds slower than the season's best for the Kenyan athletes.

The local and then national newspapers began to write stories about the asylum immigrant who was a gold medal prospect. One week before the games, national newspapers printed Commonwealth Games special supplements with sections on selected athletes. Aiyasha featured in most of them.

The articles talked not only about Aiyasha's chances of winning a gold medal for England, but about Aiyasha's appeal as well, as indicated by their headlines:

"Let's back Aiyasha for gold and get her orphans back to school"

"Give orphans their aid back by backing Aiyasha"

"Aiyasha aims for track gold and to get orphans' futures back on track"

"Back Aiyasha's appeal: give orphans their futures back"

"Aiyasha's appeal: can she be our golden girl AND orphan saviour?"

The appeal fund took off. The target was reached on the first day of the games. And it continued to grow.

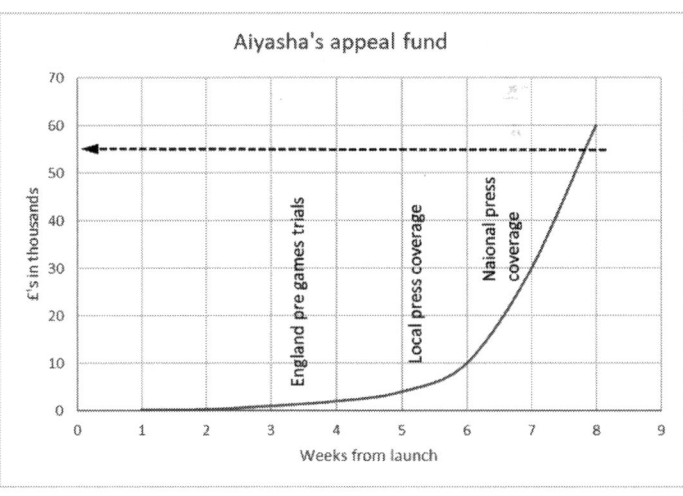

Aiyasha won a silver medal in the 10,000 metres and a gold medal in an exciting 5,000 metres, where she overtook the two Kenyan favourites in the final straight with 50 metres to go.

She was very proud of her medals. But she was prouder still of the appeal fund which had passed its target.

'Elah,' she said. 'I'm so happy that schooling for the Bundu Bunch has been secured through the appeal fund. My dreams of a bright future for them all are alive again.'

I'm not sure what dreams she had, if any, about my future.

BOOK III

Aiyasha's Magical Legacy

Contents

Prologue

Miss Gooday gave me the book called *Cry, The Beloved Country* at my school in England. The story is about South Africa. And it made me think about my own beloved country.

As an orphan and an exile, I do cry for my beloved country and my beloved Bundami valley where I was born. I miss the bright open sky, the maize fields, the river and the mountains where I spent my early years with my seven fellow orphans, who called themselves the Bundu Bunch.

Initawse

But I cry also, as Khumalo did in the book, for the people of my beloved country who are divided by privilege and poverty. Privilege corrupts the minds and actions of the most fortunate few. Poverty limits the potential of the less fortunate many.

This story tells how Aiyasha went beyond crying and took up the challenge of changing things in my beloved country of Initawse.

Chapter 1

Mixed fortunes

I'm Elah. Six years had passed since Aiyasha and I first arrived at Petranians College for Girls, in the north of England, as refugees. I was in my third year of prep school and Aiyasha was in the last year of her MSc in sport and exercise science at Leeds Beckett University. For both of us, things were looking good.

We had left behind seven fellow orphans in our homeland in the Bundami valley. Thanks to a scholarship and then a successful crowdfunding appeal by Aiyasha's friends, they were also doing well and were preparing for their O-level exams.

However, for most of our neighbours in the Bundami valley, things were not looking good at all. In the aftermath of countrywide lockdowns to contain the spread of a virus disease, businesses in town had closed, builders had no work, tourists were not visiting and prices in the shops were rising. On top of this, there had been a long dry spell and the maize cobs were small and thin. The maize storage cribs in every household had been empty for months after the previous season's poor harvest, and they would remain empty.

In the latest letter Aiyasha and I received from the Bundu Bunch, Sipho wrote:

> 'Families who previously relied on wages from jobs in town, or part-time work for builders or as tourist guides, now have no income at all. Those with government jobs have continued to receive their salaries. Meyego has been supplementing his government salary by selling food that has been given to communities by donors concerned about the plight of the poor.'

In his letter, Sipho went on to describe the situation for some of their friends from poor families. 'We were all very distressed to find so many of our friends suffering from starvation. They were like skeletons. They were listless and lethargic. They did not want to join in the games they usually played with us such as football or volleyball, and they no longer sang their songs or skipped or ran. They lay down under shady trees and slept or just stared.'

The letter ended with a request. 'Aiyasha, please can you speak to the trustees of the Aiyasha Orphans Appeal Fund to see if the charity could send money to buy food for the most-needy families?'

The Aiyasha Orphans Appeal Fund was set up to manage the donations received from the successful crowdfunding appeal. Olivia and Audrey, who had been to Bundami with a school trip seven years previously, were the trustees of the fund. They knew the situation of the families there and remembered how unfair their headman was. They agreed to send money, but told the Bundu Bunch they needed to find out how many families needed help.

* * *

Monica is the eldest of the Bundu Bunch. She is now fifteen. She organised the Bundu Bunch to go in pairs to visit all the households in the Bundami valley. The visiting groups were:

Langa and Luke (the inventors)

Sipho and Jabu (brother and sister, reporter and playmaker, respectively)

Sakhile and Jacob, with Pele (scientist, zoologist and pet mongoose).

By the end of the first week, all the families in the valley had been visited by one of the groups. When the groups came together to report their findings, they discovered that, out of the 78 families in Bundami,

53 were not getting any of the food aid because they did not have any money with which to buy it from Meyego.

The Bundu Bunch were angry to learn that so many families in their valley were not getting access to the food aid they so desperately needed.

Luke said, 'We must go to the donor and tell them their aid is not getting to the families who need it most. We must get them to confront Meyego and demand that these families get their fair share.'

But Sakhile expressed caution. 'We have to be careful,' she said. 'The donor may stop giving any food to our community if they are told it is not being fairly distributed. This would make Meyego very cross and he would surely take it out on us and the most-needy families.'

Jabu came up with the solution. As usual, she had a plan all worked out and she explained it like this.

'We should ask Aiyasha and Elah to speak to their teacher, Miss Gooday. I think she became good friends with Dr Shongwe, who was at the clinic when Miss Gooday took Aiyasha and Elah there after they had been poisoned. He helped to save their lives. If Dr Shongwe is willing to help, we can send money to him and ask him to buy food and take it to the orphan hut, where the needy families can come and collect it.'

Miss Gooday and Dr Shongwe communicated by email and it was all set up within three days. Before they returned to school, the Bundu Bunch visited the needy families and explained when they must go to the orphan hut to collect the food from Dr Shongwe. They also explained to them that they were to keep this a secret from others in the community, and especially from headman Meyego.

Aiyasha said to me, 'Elah, I am so pleased with how the Bundu Bunch have responded to the needs of their poor neighbours in Bundami and the way they have devised of assisting them.'

'Yes,' I said. 'But what about similar poor families in the other communities of Initawse?'

'You are right,' responded Aiyasha. 'But there are limited funds in the Appeal Fund and the Bundu Bunch cannot be everywhere.'

I said, 'It is so sad that the privileged few in our country are so selfish.'

Aiyasha looked at me and slowly shook her head. 'Elah,' she said. 'Its not the people in our country that are the problem. It is the system that is wrong. Remember the book you told me about. You told me that is what Khumalo came to realise in his beloved country.'

'Yes,' I replied, 'but how can you or anyone change the whole system?'

I had laid down a challenge.

Aiyasha took it up. That determined look came into her eyes, the look I knew so well. She said, quietly and slowly, 'I will change the system. I will turn it around.'

Chapter 2

Blood loyalty

It had been four years since Aiyasha had won silver and gold medals in the 5,000 and 10,000 metres at the Commonwealth Games. Now, she was training again for the delayed Olympics to be held the following year. The previous year had been frustrating for her, as she felt she had trained hard for nothing. But I persuaded her to keep going. I told her that I believed in her and I wanted her to be an Olympic champion, not just for herself but also for all those who had supported her. I had exams coming up and took my books to the trackside to give as much support as I could.

During one training session, something interesting happened about which Aiyasha and I had very divided views. I was worried it may distract her from concentrating on her training. It had the opposite effect.

* * *

Sporting success is a strange thing. At least, it does strange things to people, especially those who lead their countries. This is especially the case for international sporting successes, and even more so for sporting successes in world championships. The Olympics is the greatest sporting competition in the world and success there is the ultimate in the eyes of country leaders.

Leaders of countries will go to great lengths, break any rules, gain any advantage and make outlandish promises if they think this will result in world sporting success for their nation. It seems that such success reflects on them and becomes their success. It's funny, really, since most of these leaders don't look as if they could make it to the finishing line in a 30-metre village egg and spoon race, let alone win a race, especially an international race, or an Olympic medal.

But there it is. And that is why Aiyasha got a visit from the Deputy Chief Headman of Initawse. He arrived at the training ground in a big embassy car with national flags fluttering on either side of the bonnet.

I stood up from my books and went over to him to say hello. However, he brushed me aside and walked straight up to Aiyasha.

'Sawubona unjani?' he said in the traditional greeting of our people.

After Aiyasha replied, he told her to stop training and to go over to a nearby table to sit and talk. I went along, but was firmly ushered away by one of his two bodyguards. The Deputy Chief talked with Aiyasha for about fifteen minutes and then left.

Aiyasha then told me what he had said.

'I bring you greetings from our Chief Headman. He has learnt with pride that you are a prospect for winning a medal at the Olympics, like you did at the Commonwealth Games. You will know that, if you wanted to, you could represent your country of birth at the Olympic Games. All you would have to do is to renounce your British citizenship and declare to the Olympic committee that you wish to represent Initawse, the place where you are from and where you were born.'

He then said, 'Aiyasha, you are a daughter of our great country, you have blood loyalty to uphold. If you decide to fulfil this loyalty, I can assure you that you will be well rewarded with a house and a car and a government job of your choosing.'

Aiyasha told the him she would think about it and let him know her answer through the Embassy.

'Well?' I asked, after she had finished. 'What is your response going to be?'

'I will run for Initawse, of course,' she said.

I was surprised. 'What about the loyalty you owe to the country that adopted you?' I asked. 'That gave you an education and gave you the chance to achieve your potential, especially as an athlete? What about the loyalty you owe to the elite training programme you have been benefiting from, your loyalty to your coaches and fellow athletes, not least Greta, your training partner?'

'I also owe a loyalty to my country of birth,' said Aiyasha.

'What?' I responded incredulously. 'You mean the country where you were poisoned, from which you had to flee, where you think the privileged few live at the expense of the many in poverty? What kind of loyalty is that?'

'Blood loyalty,' said Aiyasha.

Aiyasha would not be moved. Her mind was made up. However, I noticed a sparkle in her eyes that had not been there for some time now, so I knew she had more than 'blood loyalty' in mind.

She continued her training harder than ever.

I'm not sure how much the time I spent trackside in support of Aiyasha detracted from my exam studies. But I passed anyway.

Chapter 3

Payback time

Aiyasha was training hard. Harder than I'd seen her train before. She wanted to win an Olympic medal, yes. But, from the look in her eyes, I knew the medal was not her main goal. The medal was a means to an end, not the end itself.

She had informed her coach, Mo Grindley, that she was going to represent Initawse. Mo Grindley agreed that Aiyasha could continue to train with the team GB squad, as there were no decent facilities in Initawse. Plus, she was good for the squad with her exceptional work ethic and positive attitude.

Aiyasha marched with the Initawse team at the opening ceremony of the Olympics. The Initawse flag was carried by a boxer and, apart from him and Aiyasha, there were two swimmers and a sprinter on the Initawse team. When the games started, Aiyasha was so focused that it was difficult to communicate with her. She went from the race track to the athletes' village and back without talking to anyone.

Aiyasha qualified for the finals of the 5,000 and 10,000 metre events quite easily. She went one better than she had done at the Commonwealth Games, winning gold in both races ahead of the Kenyans in second and third places.

This was the first time Initawse had had a finalist in any event. It was their first medal. And two gold medals put them ahead of all the other African countries and many rich countries in the medals table.

As he had expected, the glory rubbed off on the Chief Headman of Initawse. He gave many interviews to the world's press about how wonderful his country was and what great people he ruled. As he watched his national flag rise above the Kenyan flags, his grin was as wide as anyone had ever seen. And the Chief revelled in this glory, not just once, but twice.

Back in Initawse, crowds gathered to cheer the Chief Headman as he stepped out of the aeroplane. But an even louder cheer went up as Aiyasha stepped out behind him.

Everywhere there were placards held and flags waved with Aiyasha's face on them. Everyone wanted to meet their golden girl. However, everyone had to wait. Aiyasha had a different priority. Her first meeting was in the executive lounge with her orphan charges, the Bundu Bunch.

* * *

Aiyasha and I were overjoyed to see our orphan family again after eight long years. None of us dreamt that these eight years would turn a fleeing outcast into a popular idol for the whole nation. But, best of all, these eight years had not changed who we were. Aiyasha was still our quiet, determined mother/carer. Monica still the assertive botanist. Jacob still the fearless animal enthusiast. Sipho still the canny observer and reporter. Jabu still the resourceful playmaker. Langa and Luke still the can-do inventors, and Sakhile still the inquisitive scientist. And, of course, there was (in Jacob's pocket) Pele, the champion striker.

We had so much to talk about that everyone else had to wait a long time to meet their golden girl.

For a whole week after her arrival, Aiyasha was rushed from one venue to the next, from one community to the next, from one company to the next, from one school to the next, from one university to the next. Everyone wanted a piece of her.

Finally, she got to meet the Chief Headman at one of his palaces. She was told the Chief was very busy and could only give her a couple of his precious minutes.

Aiyasha entered the Chief's office and, after the formal introductions were over, she said what was on her mind.

'I have come to remind you about the promises you made to me when I was deciding whether to represent Initawse.'

'Ah, yes. Let me see. A house and a car, wasn't it?' responded the Chief, without looking up from his desk.

'And a job.'

'Oh, yes, and a job as well,' said the Chief, waving his hand dismissively. 'See my Finance Minister about the house and car, and my Human Resources Officer about the job.'

Finally, he looked up. 'Now, I really must get on with finalising my travel schedule for the next two months. You wouldn't believe how many invitations I have had from heads of state. I love these state visits, where they treat you like Caesar. And, I have not been to most of the countries before.

'All these invitations are because Initawse is in the top ten per cent of countries in the world on the medals table and everyone is wanting to be associated with us. So much for those people from the development agencies who said my objective of being the equivalent of a First World country by 2030 was unachievable. Here we are, and here is the evidence of our achievement: higher in the medals table than Ireland, Singapore, Norway, Israel, Austria, Portugal, Finland, and India.

'So, please, if that is all, let me get on with this important work for our country.'

'Not quite all, Chief Headman,' said Aiyasha, who

had listened very patiently to the Chief's monologue. 'You said any job in your government.'

'Yes, yes, let the Human Resources office know what you have chosen.'

Aiyasha was still not quite finished. 'The job I have chosen is in the Ministry of Education. But the appointment will need to be signed off by you. If you are going to be away for two months, that means a long delay for me.'

The Chief Headman looked up briefly, but didn't say anything.

'Please,' continued Aiyasha, 'can you sign and seal the prepared undertaking I have here to honour the promise you made as a condition of my representing Initawse in the Olympics. This is just to ensure no difficulties are brought up while you are away. You know what these civil servants are like in these matters.'

'Just so, just so. Let me look at it,' said the Chief Headman, beckoning for the papers to be given to him.

He took the papers. He looked at them quickly and signed both copies. He then asked his secretary to stamp them with the seal of the office of the Chief Headman. One copy was given back to Aiyasha.

'Thank you, Chief Headman,' said Aiyasha. 'I do hope you have a very enjoyable trip around the world. Would you like to take my two gold medals with you, to remind your hosts of the high status of our wonderful country?'

'That's kind of you, Aiyasha, but I have pictures of the flags at the award ceremony,' the Chief Headman replied. 'I think that will be enough and I would hate for your gold medals to be stolen. There is a lot of crime in some of these so-called First World countries, you know.'

With that, the meeting was over and Aiyasha allowed herself a small smile as she walked out of the Chief Headman's palace.

* * *

When Aiyasha told me what had taken place, I was dumbstruck.

'How can the Chief Headman claim his country is equivalent to a First World country,' I said, 'when we have the highest HIV prevalence in the world, the fifth highest infant mortality rate, no welfare system and two-thirds of our people live in poverty?'

Aiyasha didn't say anything, but my words did not remove the smile from her face.

Chapter 4

Outmanoeuvred

The Chief Headman began his schedule of state visits the next day. While he was enjoying the attention and lavish hospitality from world leaders, Aiyasha began to apply what she had learnt from the teacher she admired most in the world. She planned to manipulate the vanity of a powerful man to her own advantage, as she had seen Miss Gooday do.

Aiyasha employed three weapons she had primed carefully, ready to be deployed. Her first weapon was Olivia and Audrey. Now young executives in a media company, they secured an interview with the Ambassador for Initawse at the London Embassy. Their pretext was that they were writing an article for a women's magazine about Initawse as a holiday travel destination. At the end of their interview and just before they left, Olivia had one more thing to say.

'Thank you, Your Excellency, for sharing with us such wonderful information about your country,' she said. 'For our women readers planning a visit, it will be an added incentive to hear of the progressive attitude of your leader in appointing your inspiring young Olympic athlete to the position of Minister for Education.'

Quickly Audrey added, 'Oh yes, in our country, famous sportspersons have had a very positive influence on policy decisions for poor children, but our Prime Minister has not yet had the courage or insight shown by your leader. Maybe he will take a lesson from your country and appoint a famous footballer as a Minister for Children?'

The Ambassador looked taken aback. 'Could I ask where you got this information from?' he asked.

'From an article in your national newspaper,' Audrey replied.

Olivia then said, 'Come on Audrey, we must go. The editor asked for the transcript of this interview to be on her desk half an hour ago. Thank you so much for your time, Your Excellency.'

They left, leaving the Ambassador with a puzzled frown on his face. He sent a briefing to the Chief Minister's office in Initawse. It was headed: 'Aiyasha's appointment to the Ministry of Education.'

* * *

Aiyasha's second weapon was Sipho. Sipho was now a trainee reporter at the national newspaper in Initawse to which Audrey had referred.

He had managed to get a late entry into that morning's edition of the paper. This article featured a picture of Aiyasha walking out of the Chief Headman's palace, with a sheet of paper in her hand clearly showing the Chief Headman's signature and the stamp of his office.

Sipho's article had extolled the virtues of the wise and forward-looking Chief Headman, who had appointed Aiyasha to the position of Minister for Education.

* * *

The third weapon in Aiyasha's arsenal was the social media skills of the Bundu Bunch. All of them had Facebook, Instagram, Twitter, and Snapchat accounts. And all of them had a wide network of 'friends' on these accounts.

They started a social media discussion on the appointment of Aiyasha as Minister for Education. Snapchat texts circulated attached to a photo of Aiyasha:

'Hey, did you see A was appointed Minister for Education?'

'Wow, that's cool, how wonderful!'

'Yes, and what a surprise for our Leader to do this.'

'So, the Chief Headman is not so bad after all!'

'At last, some recognition of young people in this country of ours.'

'Yes, and of women also.'

The Deputy Chief Headman was hounded by the national and international press to confirm that Aiyasha had indeed been appointed Minister for Education. Before he had left for his tour, the Chief Headman had not mentioned such a thing to his deputy, so he was not able to give a definitive response without speaking with the Chief Headman.

The Chief Headman was currently on the small Island of Vanuatu on his way to New Zealand. The phone reception was not very good. When they finally connected, the deputy asked the Chief if he had given Aiyasha the job of Minister for Education.

'Yes, that is right,' said the Chief. 'She asked for a job in the Ministry of Education and I said she could have it.'

The line was not good. The deputy had to make sure that what he had just heard was correct.

'Did you say you gave her the job of Minister *for* Education or a job *in* the Ministry of Education?'

'Yes, right first time,' responded the Chief, who really had not heard the question very clearly, but was keen to get to his next engagement: a traditional grass skirt dance display and banquet.

The line went dead.

The deputy then remembered the article in the national paper with the picture of Aiyasha holding a signed piece of paper. He went to the office of the Chief Headman to check on what had been written down on the matter.

The secretary showed him the agreement, which clearly stated that the Chief Headman had given Aiyasha the job of Minister for Education.

So, that was how the appointment was confirmed to the national and international press and the people of Initawse. And how it came about that Aiyasha started her work as Minister for Education from her large office, with her large ministerial car and her well-guarded house in the capital.

This all happened while the Chief Headman was still on his world tour. By the time he returned, Aiyasha was firmly in position and making herself the most popular minister in his cabinet.

I still believe that the Chief Headman had not intended this to happen and that he knew he had been lax in not reading the agreement papers properly. He knew he had been outmanoeuvred by Aiyasha. However, if he did think that, then he was not displeased with the outcome. On his arrival back in Initawse, he held a press conference.

'I have called this press conference to clear up issues around the appointment of Aiyasha as Minister for Education,' he began. 'There seems to have been speculation about this decision and my intent. I can assure you my motivation is to promote the lives and well-being of our young people, especially those from disadvantaged families, for whom Aiyasha is a role model.'

The news media at home and abroad applauded what they described as this bold and imaginative leadership. The Chief's government was more popular than ever.

I could imagine him saying to himself, 'Actually, it's fine. I've come out well from my mistake that nobody knows about but me. And she is only a young girl heading up an inefficient and unimportant Ministry. She can't do me any harm.'

Chapter 5

Turning the tables

Aiyasha gave it a couple of months to become established in her post. She implemented some popular initiatives, like a review of teachers' pay and conditions, improving the quality of school lunches and allowing parents to have more say in how schools were run.

Only then did she start to implement the changes that she had really come here to make. These were the changes she had trained and run so hard for. The changes she had dreamt about from when she was teaching her orphans in secret, at her briefcase classes deep in the Bundami forest. The changes that would lead to her ambition 'to turn the tables'.

Aiyasha began by going to all the communities in Initawse to discuss the need for orphans and children from the poorest families to attend preschool. At each community, she selected two members to become preschool teachers. Training was organised for all these teachers while a preschool building was constructed in each community.

At each community, Aiyasha called a meeting and spoke to all the members.

'The new government preschool in your community is for your most disadvantaged children,' she said. 'The places in these preschools are only for your children who are living in households where nobody has a job, and where they are unable to send their children to private preschools because they cannot pay the fees. You, the community, must select the children who will go to the preschools.'

Like the Bundu Bunch, the disadvantaged children selected by their communities gleefully took the opportunity to learn new things and have the wonderful world of stories, books and puzzles opened up to them for the first time.

At the start of the following year, there was a big demand for places at Aiyasha's new preschools. Everyone had seen that the children from the Aiyasha preschools did much better than children from private preschools and were all at the top of their classes in their primary schools. People started calling Aiyasha's preschools the 'Golden Future' preschools, after the medals Aiyasha had won. The Golden Future preschools were better run, had better books, puzzles and games, had more committed teachers and keener students than other preschools.

Aiyasha had to revisit all the communities and remind them that only orphans and other children from the poorest families were allowed to go to the new preschools, because these children had no books in their homes and needed this early learning opportunity the most. This caused a lot of grumbling from the privileged families. They said that they wanted *their* children to attend the Golden Future preschools and would pay the highest level of fees for this to happen.

Aiyasha's reply was a resounding 'NO'. The policy of the Ministry was that the Golden Future preschools were for children from the poorest families only. The grumblings from the privileged continued, but the majority of the community members supported the principle of attendance at the Golden Future preschools.

The grumblings from the privileged families got even louder when Aiyasha implemented the next part of her 'turning the tables' policy.

Some of the high schools in Initawse were better than others. They had the best teachers and best facilities. They also had the highest fees. Only children from privileged families went to these schools. These schools were half full of dumb pupils from rich families who failed at all the exams, however good the teachers were.

Aiyasha changed this. Only pupils who passed their exams could go to these schools. But, more importantly, they no longer had to be from a privileged family to go to these schools, because the Ministry of Education would pay their way.

After a few years, these schools went from being full of privileged children to being mostly full of children from poor families who had been to the Golden Future preschools and done better than privileged children at exams.

The tables had been turned. For the first time, the privileged were experiencing an inequality that was a disadvantage for them.

Chapter 6

Privileged protest

All the privileged families, including those in government jobs, went to see the Chief Headman to complain.

'Because of the action of your Minister for Education,' said one parent, 'we cannot get our children into the best schools any more. You must make Aiyasha change her new policy or sack her and get another Minister for Education. It is just not fair that our children cannot go to the best schools. Our children have the right to have access to the best education.'

The Chief Minister told Aiyasha what these representatives were saying. 'You will have to change your policy. These are the most important people in the country and we have to do what they say. We must be fair to their children and enable them to go to the best schools.'

Aiyasha refused.

'No,' she said. 'They are not the most important people in the country. The most important people for the future of our country are the ones that are doing best in their exams, and they are the ones we are accepting to the best schools.'

And she said 'No' again. 'No, it is not unfair for children from privileged families to be unable to buy places at the best schools. We need to be fair to all children, not just the ones from privileged families, and that is what my policy is doing. All children have an equal right to a good education, and while we still have some schools that are better than others, the children doing best at exams will go to those schools as this is the best thing for the country. I will not change my policy. It is the best for the future of our country.'

The Chief Headman replied, 'If you will not change, Aiyasha, I will have to ask you to resign. Otherwise, I will sack you.'

Aiyasha stood her ground. 'I will not resign. And you know you cannot sack me. If you do, I will speak out about how I tricked you into appointing me, and you could not live with that. My schools policy stays and you will come to see that it will be for the long-term benefit of our country.'

The Chief Headman knew that he relied on the privileged families to keep his position. Aiyasha had to go. But, more than that, she had to go silently to avoid more protests and potential unrest in the country.

Chapter 7

Disappearance

I was really excited about my visit to London to stay with Olivia and Audrey at their flat in Oval Mansions. They had invited me to discuss my university application. Well, that was the excuse. For me, any reason to go and stay with them would do.

Audrey was now an executive in a finance firm. Olivia was a journalist with a weekly news magazine. I had just finished my final year at Petranians College for Girls. I hadn't been able to stop thinking about my trip ever since my last exam.

And my stay with these two young professionals, in the most exciting city in the world, lived up to all my expectations.

Olivia met me at St Pancras station.

'Elah!' she shouted from the end of the platform. She threw her arms around me, then took one of my bags and led me to the underground. We squeezed into the crowded tube and rattled our way to the Oval tube station. From there, it was a short walk across Westminster Bridge to the flat.

Just that short trip through bustling, busy London with Olivia was inspiring. But it was their flat that blew me away. From one side, you looked out onto the Oval cricket ground. What a surprise. In the middle of one of the largest, busiest cities in the world, I was looking down on a genial green grass garden of tranquillity amidst a ceaseless cacophony cascading around the city's concrete castles.

On the other side of the flat, you looked out at the London Eye and the Houses of Parliament across the river. At night, you saw the pods of the Eye slowly moving across the sky and the Houses of Parliament reflected in the river. It was magical.

And it all got better and better as the days went by. I got to accompany both girls to their places of work and marvelled at their open-plan glass offices. And I got to meet many of their friends. I can't remember what we discussed about my university application, or whether we even looked at it, but I do remember it as a wonderful week of discovery, laughter and fun.

On the last night of my stay, Olivia received an agitated telephone call from Jabu, who was ringing from the capital of Initawse.

'Have you heard the news?' Jabu asked. 'Aiyasha has disappeared. She is not in her office, nor at her house. Nobody has seen her since Thursday, so it's been four days now. We are very worried that something bad has happened to her.'

'OK,' responded Olivia. 'Slow down and tell us why you think something bad has happened to her.'

Jabu explained what had been happening in Initawse over the previous few weeks.

'The privileged families have been protesting about Aiyasha's education programme,' she began. 'They have been calling for Aiyasha to be sacked. But most of the people support Aiyasha's Golden Future preschools for orphans and poor children, and the ability this gives them to compete equally for places at the best schools. Most people think this is fair. There have been protests by privileged parents and clashes in the streets between the privileged families and others.'

Jabu then explained that the Chief Headman had called for calm. He said he would have a meeting with representatives of the two sides and with Aiyasha, to decide what was to be done about her position and her education policies. That had been on Thursday the previous week. Aiyasha had not been seen after that meeting, she had disappeared.

Jabu went on, 'The government says they have no idea what happened to Aiyasha and they are not responsible for her disappearance. They say they will mount a police hunt to find her.'

At this point, Jabu started to sob. 'We don't have any confidence in the police and suspect there will be a cover-up to protect whoever is responsible. We are really worried that Aiyasha has been abducted by the privileged side, and has been injured, or even killed.'

Jabu ended with an emotional plea. 'You must help us find her and make sure she hasn't come to any harm.'

I looked at Olivia and Audrey. They were nodding to each other.

Audrey took the phone from Olivia. 'Don't worry, Jabu,' she said calmly. 'Of course we will help find Aiyasha. We will talk about it and let you know what we plan to do. In the meantime, gather whatever additional information you can about Aiyasha's last-known movements. We will get back by phone to Sipho, as we have his number at the newspaper. Goodbye for now.'

Olivia and Audrey cancelled their plans for the party they were going to take me to on my last night. They called their friends to tell them something had come up and that they didn't want to be disturbed that evening. They then ordered a curry takeaway and we settled down in the lounge to take stock of the situation and to try to come up with a plan of action.

Chapter 8

Investigation

It didn't take us long to come up with a plan to help Jabu and the rest of the Bundu Bunch find Aiyasha. Olivia and Sipho were the obvious ones to take the lead. Olivia persuaded the editor of the weekly magazine she worked for to send her out to investigate the disappearance of Initawse's Minister for Education and write a story for the magazine. After all, Aiyasha was an international star, being a double gold medal winner, and there was a lot of interest in what had become of her. Also, Olivia knew Aiyasha and she had visited the country and knew the people there.

Sipho also persuaded the editor of his newspaper to let him team up with Olivia and report on the case for the national paper. The last time they had seen each other was when Olivia was in the sixth form and Sipho was about to start primary school. That was sixteen years ago. When the 23-year-old trainee reporter and the 31-year-old magazine executive met at the airport in Initawse, it was as if they had been colleagues all their working lives. After their gleeful greeting and exclamations about how wonderful it was to meet again, they got down to planning their investigation.

The two journalists started by collecting as much information as they could about Aiyasha's last-known whereabouts in the days before her disappearance. The first person they interviewed was Aiyasha's secretary in the Ministry of Education.

Aiyasha's secretary confirmed that Aiyasha had had a meeting with the Chief Headman on the Thursday and a followup meeting had been set up with all the headmen for Friday. But Aiyasha had not attended the Friday meeting. The last time Aiysha's secretary had seen her was when she had left the office on Thursday evening.

Next, they went to see Aiyasha's driver. The driver told them he had taken Aiyasha to her house on Thursday evening and had been asked to pick her up from there the next morning at 9 am.

The driver said, 'I was surprised when Aiyasha asked me to drive her to Bundami and not to her office. I took her there and she directed me to an old hut at the end of the valley.'

He continued, 'Aiyasha then told me I could leave her there. She said I must drive back to the office and wait there until she contacted me. That is what I did and I never heard from her again.'

Olivia asked the driver, 'What did Aiyasha take with her and what was she wearing?'

'She was wearing her normal office clothes,' he replied. 'She had her briefcase with her and a small bag. I don't know what was in the bag, except for her running shoes, which I saw her put in the bag as I arrived to collect her.'

Next, Sipho asked the driver how Aiyasha seemed the day he took her to Bundami. The driver said she seemed normal, although she was coughing more than usual.

'What do you mean by more than usual?' asked Sipho.

'Well, she had developed a cough over the past couple of weeks,' replied the driver, 'and it seemed to be getting worse.'

Olivia and Sipho thanked the driver, and came away from the interview with a lot of questions in their minds: Had Aiyasha been forced to go in the ministerial car? If so, by whom and why, and where did they take her? Did Aiyasha actually go to Bundami? Had it been her own decision? If so, why did she go there?

It took Olivia and Sipho three days to get a meeting with the Chief Headman. When they did, he was very brusque with them and told them they had ten minutes at the most.

They asked the Chief Headman what he had discussed with Aiyasha at his meeting with her on the Thursday before she disappeared. He said it was about the protests of the privileged people, which included his ministers and government employees. He said he asked her to change her education policies, but she had refused to do so.

'So you had a disagreement, then?' asked Olivia. 'Did you threaten her in any way to make her change her mind?'

'I did not,' said the Chief Headman.

'Did you abduct her to get her out of the way so you could change her policies?' asked Olivia more forcefully.

'I did not,' was the response.

Sipho then questioned the Chief Headman, but more calmly. 'Now she is gone, do you intend to change her policies?'

'Er, yes … I mean, no, probably not, not immediately,' was the hesitant reply.

'Why not?' said Sipho. 'Was that not the reason why you arranged to get her out of the way?'

Now the Chief Headman was angry. 'I made no such arrangement! I had nothing to do with her disappearance. I will not answer any more of your questions. My secretary will show you out.'

'He is hiding something, he is not telling us everything,' said Olivia, as they left.

'I agree,' said Sipho. 'Things don't add up. There are two other places we need to look, to see if we can find any trace of her to confirm the driver's story. We need to look at her ministerial car and visit the orphan hut in Bundami.'

* * *

In both these places, Sipho and Olivia found the sort of evidence that they had hoped they would never find. Evidence of foul play.

In the well of the front seat of the car, and on the floor of the orphan hut, next to where Aiyasha used to sleep, there were spots of blood.

With the help of Sakhile's contacts through her genomics work, they managed to get samples of the blood tested for DNA. Sure enough, the blood was from Aiyasha.

Olivia and Sipho took these results to the police and asked them to open a murder inquiry. It certainly looked as though Aiyasha had been taken by force, but the police said there was not enough evidence of murder and, without the body, they would not consider launching a murder investigation.

Olivia and Sipho then focused their investigation on finding Aiyasha's body. They were convinced she had been abducted and murdered. They interviewed more than 100 witnesses, all of whom said they had seen Aiyasha after the Friday. Some of these reported sightings were at the southern border, some at the western border and some in Bundami itself.

Then they got their breakthrough. A community member in Bundami said they had seen Aiyasha outside the orphan hut on the Friday afternoon. Another said they had seen Meyego coming from the direction of the orphan hut later that evening. This witness said Meyego was looking at a round disc in his hand that was shining brightly in the late afternoon sun.

One week after Aiyasha's disappearance, Sipho and Olivia confronted Meyego with their damming evidence.

Meyego first denied seeing Aiyasha or going to the orphan hut the previous week. When he was shown fresh footprints coming from the hut that matched his large boots, he admitted he had been there. He said he had gone to check if anyone was there, but found nobody.

When asked about the gleaming object in his hand, he shrugged his shoulders and said the reflection must have been from his gold watch.

Olivia and Sipho were dejected when they called the Bundu Bunch from Sipho's office later that day to report on their findings. They were convinced Aiyasha had been abducted and may even have been killed. But there was no firm evidence to back up their suspicions.

Reluctantly, they all agreed there was nothing more they could do, and agreed they would catch up again soon.

* * *

Olivia was called back to London by her editor. Aiyasha's whereabouts, or that of her body, was no closer to being discovered than when Olivia had left for Bundami four weeks ago. Public interest had been overtaken by other events in the world.

When Olivia got back to the flat that she shared with Audrey, she threw her case onto the floor and sat down at the kitchen table with her head in her hands. That is how Audrey found her when she returned from her office. The girls looked sadly at each other and held hands and cried.

'I feel we have let Aiyasha down,' sobbed Olivia.

'Yes, and the Bundu Bunch and Elah, as well,' said Audrey.

* * *

Back in the capital city of Initawse, Sipho was equally as upset. They had worked so hard. They had followed up every lead and interviewed hundreds of people, but had nothing to show for it. The people of

Initawse were getting on with their lives again and talking about other things. Their government was changing. The first leadership elections were coming up. Life was exciting. Everybody was feeling better off and they were all moving ahead together as one.

Then, out of the blue, came a small glimmer of hope for the Bundu Bunch. Audrey received an envelope in the post, addressed to the treasurer of the Aiyasha Orphans Appeal Fund. The envelope contained a payment demand and part of a page from an ABC letters book. The page showed a map of Africa with numbers written over some of the countries.

Audrey thought this must have come from Aiyasha's ABC book. When she contacted me for my opinion, I immediately confirmed this was the very page Aiyasha used to teach me about the different countries we travelled across on our way to seek asylum in England.

If a regular payment is set up and no attempt is made to trace the account, Aiyasha's wellbeing will be guaranteed. Monica eight oranges.

The payment demand was for £400 to be paid each month into a bank account in Johannesburg. The note also contained a strangely worded warning attached to the heading of the *Sowetan* newspaper.

Olivia looked at the newspaper clipping with the note attached. 'This is from three days ago. The message must have been couriered to London and then put in the post to get here today.'

'So, Aiyasha is alive and well,' I said, clapping my hands.

'Is she, though?' said Audrey, with a frown. 'The page from the ABC book indicates the message has to do with Aiyasha. But it could have been sent by someone who has killed Aiyasha, torn out the page from the ABC book and sent it to make us think she is alive. I agree, the writing looks like Aiyasha's, but writing style can be copied.'

'I think the page is there to make us think of Aiyasha's Briefcase Classes,' replied Olivia. 'I'm wondering what the last three words of the message attached to the newspaper clipping mean. I think we need to ask the Bundu Bunch if they have any idea how they could be related to their ABC classes.'

I set up a Zoom video call to Sipho, who had managed to get Sakhile and Jabu to join him. I showed them the newspaper clipping with the note attached and the page from the ABC book and explained what

Olivia was thinking about the message being related to their ABC classes.

'Those last three words don't make any sense to us,' I said.

Sipho, Sakhile and Jabu looked at each other and nodded their heads.

Sipho spoke for all three of them. 'It makes perfect sense to us,' he said. 'At our classes, one of us was responsible each day for writing the date on the ground next to Aiyasha and then rubbing it out at the end of the class. On Mondays it was me, Tuesdays it was Monica, Wednesdays it was Jabu, Thursdays it was Jacob, Fridays it was Sakhile, Saturdays it was Luke, and Sundays it was Langa.'

'Yes,' said Sakhile, unable to keep the excitement out of her voice. 'And, for each month of the year we had identified a fruit to be associated with it. December was lychees, January was mango and so on. And September was orange.'

'So you see,' said Jabu, 'the last three words mean Tuesday, 8th September. The very date of the newspaper clip that the note was attached to. Nobody else would have known to write those words, which shows Aiyasha was definitely alive on that day and the message is from her. We must do as she asks.'

Audrey set up the payment. Although this did not solve anything about Aiyasha's whereabouts, it gave us all some hope to hang on to and encouragement to keep going with our lives.

Chapter 9

Bundu Bunch breakthroughs

I followed in Olivia's footsteps and chose to study Philosophy at London University. By the time I had started my university course, the Bundu Bunch orphans had all received their degrees and were immersed in their new jobs.

I followed their progress with interest and fascination because, as you will see, they all made valuable contributions to the advancement of their country. To me, though, the most amazing thing was that their achievements complemented each other. Their initiatives and enterprise came together, just as I remember when they explored the wonders of their Bundami valley and named themselves the Bundu Bunch.

As an agronomist in the Research Division of the Ministry of Agriculture, Monica pioneered the technique of precision placement of nutrients in the soil to enable plant seeds to grow to their maximum potential. By estimating the exact nutrient requirement of a plant in a given soil, farmers were able to halve the amount of fertiliser they used and get a higher yield at the same time.

While Monica was field testing her technique, Luke and Langa were developing the first solar-powered seed planter in the world. The planter could be pre-programmed to work on any field shape and soil type and enabled farmers to claim carbon credits by avoiding the use of diesel powered tractors.

Meanwhile, Sakhile was working in her genomics laboratory. She had discovered a gene in pearl millet that enabled it to pause development when there was a lack of rain, and then to continue to develop and grow when rain came again. This enabled farmers to produce well-formed grain in drought conditions.

Using the CRISPR gene-editing technique, Sakhile had managed to introduce what she called the 'pause gene' into maize. She explained the rationale for her research as follows. 'Our normal maize will continue to develop and produce cobs even when there is no rain. But the whole plant remains small and, although the cobs are formed, the kernels in them are small and few.'

She continued, 'You see, the point of introducing the "pause gene" is to enable the plant to halt its development during a dry spell and then continue to grow and develop once rains come again.'

The result was that Sakhile's modified maize produced good cobs, even after a prolonged dry spell. This meant that farmers got a good crop every year, instead of only when there was a sustained rainy season.

Jabu had graduated with a degree in business administration and was employed as a manager of a small social research institute in the capital of Initawse. When she learnt of the work that Monica, Luke, Langa and Sakhile were doing, she recognised the need for an integrated research institute to bring together the different discoveries being made by researchers.

She submitted a proposal for the expansion of the social research institute to the managing director. The managing director told her it was a good idea, but the problem was funding. They needed money to expand the building, to employ staff to support researchers and to pay researchers to design and implement research programmes. They needed a lot of money.

When Jabu wrote to me about her ambitions and the finance problem, I immediately thought of Audrey. She was working in investment banking in London, and London is the world centre of capital markets.

Audrey was onto it like a flash. Within three months, she had secured venture capital commitments for the project amounting to over £5,000,000.

Jabu was able to build her expanded research institution. She called it the 'Centre for the Advancement of New Discovery Options'. It soon came to be known as the CANDO centre. She told me later how much she liked that. She said, 'It reminds me of our Bundu Bunch motto that we developed in those early days in the Bundami valley.'

It was at the CANDO centre that the work of Monica, Luke and Langa, and of Sakhile were brought together with the most amazing results.

Luke and Langa adapted their solar-powered planter to become a combined planting and fertilising machine. Their machine adopted Monica's precision nutrient placement technique. And, of course, the maize seed that the machine planted was the variety which included Sakhile's pause gene.

Farmers called it a miracle. They now managed to harvest a good crop in nearly all years, even poor rainfall ones. They used half the fertiliser and saved on the costs of operating tractors for planting and fertilising. Never again did farmers in Bundami experience empty maize cribs.

But this was not all. Jabu's CANDO centre applied for carbon credits on account of the fossil fuel savings through use of less fertiliser, and the use of solar power instead of tractor power for planting and fertilising. Maize farmers in Initawse received payouts from the carbon credit scheme which more than covered their costs of seed, fertiliser and hire of the solar planter/ fertiliser machine. No wonder they called it a miracle.

Jacob, meanwhile, was involved with another miracle brought about by the CANDO centre. This was not a farming miracle, but a health miracle.

Jacob had set up a snake farm for tourists, but he also used the facilities on his farm to investigate how Pele and other mongooses managed to win their fights against cobras and other snakes. He noticed that, although the mongooses dodged most snake strikes, they did not avoid being bitten by snakes completely. However, they were unaffected by the venom. He discovered that they excreted an oily substance onto their fur, which neutralised the venom.

And Jacob's discovery led to something else much more significant for Initawse and the whole world. The two staff Jacob had employed on his snake farm to work with the mongooses were HIV positive. Jacob agreed to give them time off every two weeks to attend the HIV clinic, where their cell counts were monitored and their drug regimes were adjusted. He was surprised to receive a visit from one of the HIV doctors three months after his new staff had joined the snake farm.

After introducing himself, the doctor said, 'I have good news about your two workers, Tenu and Sven, who have been coming to my clinic. Both of them have made remarkable recoveries from their HIV infections. Their immune systems have not only cleared the active virus in their bodies, but have also developed the capacity to prevent the generation of new copies of the virus. This is unprecedented in my experience and I wanted to learn a bit more about their working environment here.'

'Tenu and Sven work in the mongoose pen,' Jacob replied. 'They have been helping in my investigations on how mongooses avoid being affected by snake venom. I use them there because they are both good at handling the mongooses. At first, they made the mongooses very nervous and they received many scratches. I was thinking of replacing them, but they have learnt how to keep the mongooses calm and have a good relationship with them now.'

'That's interesting,' said the doctor. 'And I understand you have been doing some research on mongoose immunity to snake venom, is that right?' Jacob confirmed that this was the case and he told the HIV doctor about the oily substance the mongooses excreted, which neutralised the venom.

'You see,' said the doctor, 'both these patients have developed a very rare type of antibody with potent neutralising activity against a broad range of HIV strains. I am wondering if there may be a link between the substance excreted by your mongooses and this rare antibody development by Tenu and Sven.'

That was the start of a large research project on the oily substance Pele and his friends excreted and its effect on the HIV virus. The project was hosted at the CANDO centre under Jabu's direction. She recruited a large team of scientists, including Sakhile, who worked on the genomics aspects of the project.

Sakhile also took the lead in adopting the messenger RNA technology to develop a successful HIV vaccine. For over 40 years, researchers around the world had been trying to develop this. Now, here was the first, developed in Initawse at the CANDO centre.

Initawse rapidly changed from having the highest rates of HIV in the world to having the lowest in all of Africa. What a turnaround.

* * *

It is often the case that formal unveiling ceremonies to mark the establishment of new institutions happen long after they are up and running. That was the case here. The newly elected Minister for Technology was a proud man as he took the stand in front of international press cameras to unveil the sign above Jabu's innovative research institution.

That man was Samu, now aged 38. He made a speech about how he knew the administrator of the centre and many of the researchers and had grown up with them in the Bundami valley. He extolled their virtues and said how proud of them he was.

Then he declared the institute officially inaugurated and pulled the string to expose the name on the plaque. The cameras clicked as the sign was revealed. It read:

CANDO

Centre for Anyone Named a Dumb Orphan

Minister Samu was smiling broadly into the cameras. Only when he heard the gasps of astonishment from the audience did he turn round to look at the sign he had unveiled.

For a moment, he looked dumfounded. Then he remembered the words that he and his friends used to chant at Jabu, Monica, Jacob, Sakhile, Luke, Langa and Sipho:

Orphans are dumb.
They don't know their letters
And can't spell their name.
Oh dear, what a shame.

As for numbers
They are a mystery for them.
Getting the answers
Is a guessing game.
Oh dear, what a shame

They look like scarecrows,
All skin and bone.
They've lost their mums
And don't accept the blame.
Oh dear, what a shame.

Samu laughed loudly. He turned back to the audience and said.

'Our orphans in Bundami were always cheeky. To my shame, as a child, I did call them dumb orphans. But they were not too dumb to miss the chance of having some fun with a bun at my expense.'

'Not just one bun, many buns,' called a heckler from the audience.

Samu was not put out. 'Yes, OK, quite a lot of buns, and I paid a high price for every one of them.'

He continued in a more serious voice. 'In those days, there was us and them. The privileged and the poor. I'm glad to say that now we are all together and the CANDO centre has contributed in no small measure to the turnaround in the fortunes of our country. I am also glad to note that we no longer have so many orphans, and none of them are dumb, thanks to our Golden Future preschools. So we can do away with this sign.'

With that, Minister Samu pulled a second cord and the real sign was revealed:

CANDO

Centre for Advancement of
New Discovery Options

Inaugurated by the Minister for Technology

After the ceremony the press and their readers had two questions. Who had planned the unveiling prank and was Minister Samu in on the plan? The answer to the first question was soon revealed and was a surprise to nobody. It was Sipho. Neither the Bundu Bunch nor Minister Samu ever revealed the truth about the second question.

I followed the press coverage on the CANDO centre from Leeds, where I had completed a postgraduate teaching course and was now deputy head of a primary school in the city. Most of the national papers and news websites contained articles about the centre and its research programmes that led the world in areas such as HIV vaccination and environmentally sustainable agriculture. Some of the articles focused on the scientists leading these programmes including Sakhile, Jacob, Monica and Luke and Langa.

I read these articles with mixed feelings. Feelings of joy of course for the international acclaim given to members of the Bundu Bunch. But I also felt sad that Aiyasha was not there to witness the fame and success of her orphan charges. I think it was the Guardian newspaper that picked up on the fact that these orphans were the very same students who had been supported by Aiyasha's highly successful Back us Orphans crowdfunding appeal launched just before the commonwealth games twenty seven years earlier. This inevitably led to speculation on what had become of Aiyasha and spawned a range of theories including kidnapping, political assassination, mental breakdown, poisoning, trauma leading to amnesia and probably others.

All this coverage on Aiyasha and her orphans brought back to me my abiding feeling of inadequacy as I compared my achievements with them. I couldn't help thinking how proud Aiyasha would be of the Bundu Bunch orphans. I so much wished she could have had reason to be equally proud of me.

Chapter 10

The stuff of legends

Sixteen years had passed since Sipho and Olivia had reluctantly closed their investigation on Aiyasha's disappearance and Olivia had gone back to London. Sipho had been promoted to deputy editor of the national newspaper. It was a hot Wednesday morning. Mid-week was usually quiet for news and Sipho was looking forward to his round of golf in the corporate golf league competition that afternoon.

His secretary knocked on the door of his posh office and entered. 'There is a poor herdboy from South Africa who says he has something to give you,' she said. 'He says he must give it to you himself, because he has a message that only you will understand.'

'OK,' said Sipho. 'Show him in.'

A small, thin boy walked slowly towards Sipho.

'Hello, what is your name?' asked Sipho.

'Angelo,' replied the boy, quietly. He held out a small piece of leather with some threads hanging from the sides.

Sipho gasped when he took hold of the old piece of leather. He recognised it. It was a patch from Aiyasha's briefcase. The one from the front, on the left. He and the rest of the Bundu Bunch had spent many hours looking at that briefcase, wondering what was going to come out of it next. He could not mistake it. The size, colour and shape meant it could be nothing else.

'Where did you get this?' asked Sipho.

'By the river which borders the Mountain Kingdom,' was the reply. 'A goat herder from the hills gave it to me at the livestock auction there. He said he would give me a goat if I took it to you and delivered the message'

'And what is the message?' enquired Sipho.

'Not here,' replied the herdboy.

'Then where?' asked Sipho. 'Where must we go for you to give me the message?'

'Nowhere,' was the answer. 'That's the message, which only the person it is intended for will understand.'

And with that, the herdboy turned around and was about to head out of the door. Sipho called him back.

However, try as he might, Sipho was not able to get another word out of the herdboy. Eventually, he had to let him go, but not before he asked his secretary to give him some bread, spread liberally with peanut butter, and an apple and some milk. Sipho also gave the herdboy a note to confirm he had received the patch and the message. The note also said Angelo should receive the payment of a goat, that he had been promised.

Sipho was excited, but baffled. Excited because this had been the first link with Aiyasha for over twelve years. But baffled, because he could not think what the message meant. His head was spinning. He had to get some help.

He knew Monica, Luke, Langa and Sakhile were on the experimental farm and out of phone range. Jacob was at an HIV conference. So Sipho rang his sister, Jabu, at the CANDO centre.

Jabu listened to Sipho. 'It must be a message from Aiyasha for us alone,' she said. 'We must keep this to ourselves.'

But Jabu was just as baffled as Sipho about what the message meant.

Then she had a good idea. 'Why don't you ask Olivia what she thinks? She was involved in the investigation of Aiyasha's disappearance with you. Maybe it will mean something to her.'

It did.

* * *

When she heard Sipho's story, Olivia knew the answer immediately.

'The Mountain Kingdom, that's the key!' she said. 'The Mountain Kingdom stretches from the Caledon River to the very top of the Drakensburg mountains. A huge dam is being developed there to bring water down to the big cities of Johannesburg and Durban. It is very remote and can only be reached by helicopter or a long pony trek. Aiyasha's message saying "not here" refers to the briefcase patch being found by the river. It means the briefcase patch did not come from the river. No, it means the briefcase is at the other source of water. And what was the other source of water for the Bundu Bunch in Bundami?'

'Of course!' cried Sipho, on the other end of the line. 'Our other source of water was up on the mountain. The briefcase is at the highland dam, at the top of the Drakensburg Mountain. And where the briefcase is, that is where Aiyasha will be.'

* * *

Olivia and Audrey packed their bags and boarded a flight to Johannesburg. It was the start of a new school year so I was not able to join them, as much as I wanted to. I learned what happened from Olivia and Audrey when they returned and from a letter Sipho wrote to me. From the airport Audrey and Olivia hired a car and drove through the Karoo desert, to meet up with the Bundu Bunch on the banks of the Caledon River. There was much hugging and exclaiming as Olivia and Audrey met the Bundu Bunch again. So much had happened since they the last time they had all been together. Wonderful things, like Aiyasha's medals, the career successes of the orphan group, the positive changes in the country of Initawse. But these were all overshadowed by the mystery of Aiyasha's disappearance.

They gradually fell quiet and looked across the river into the Mountain Kingdom, letting their eyes scan the hills up to the top of the mighty Drakensburg mountains. They had the feeling that, at last, they were going to find out what had become of Aiyasha.

For the first ten miles, they took a combi bus across a plain to the foothills of the mountain which rose above them like a wall. From there, they hired ponies and started the three-day trek to the site of the Highland Water Project. On arrival, they went to the manager's office. Here, they were greeted warmly and directed to the guest house, where they were relieved to be able to lie down on soft beds and take the pressure off their very sore bottoms.

In his letter Sipho wrote, 'If you have ever ridden on a pony for three days, Elah, you will know the wonder of being able to stretch out on a soft bed. We all slept soundly.'

The next day, they had a meeting with the manager to explain why they had come to this remote project site. As they told the story of Aiyasha's disappearance, the manager nodded his head slowly.

When they had finished, the manager said, 'Yes, I know of the person of whom you speak, although I have never seen her. She lives in an old, abandoned mission compound in the next valley. Money is sent from London each month to our head office in Johannesburg for food and provisions, which I send to her from our project store. Nobody else knows about this arrangement, and I was asked to keep it to myself, which I have done until now. Yesterday, Aiyasha sent me a message that she expected you would be coming and I could reveal her whereabouts.'

'This was great to hear,' wrote Sipho, 'but, oh dear! It meant getting onto those ponies again for another day's trek to the next valley. Of course, we were all keen to get going, despite the insult this was going to do to our bottoms. That was a small price to pay for the chance of seeing Aiyasha again.'

After another painful ten hours on the ponies, they crested the last ridge and looked down on the valley below. They spotted the mission compound immediately. Nestled against a clump of wattle trees was a brick building with a wooden cross above the doorway.

Jacob led the way down the hill to the compound. Near the brick building was a mud-and-stick house with a thatched roof. Sitting outside and tending a cooking pot was an old lady, thin and frail, with white hair.

As soon as the old lady looked up, they knew they were looking at Aiyasha. Her eyes were as bright and determined as ever. They sparkled as she saw the Bundu Bunch and Audrey and Olivia. She smiled warmly at them.

'I've been waiting for you to come,' said Aiyasha in a soft voice. 'It's lovely to see you all. Thank you for coming and for understanding my message.'

In his letter Sipho wrote, 'Elah, we were all in shock. None of us knew what to say. We just stood there in front of Aiyasha for a while. Then, in turn, each of us knelt in front of her and held her hands and kissed her cheek gently, carefully and lovingly.'

Aiyasha pointed to the pot in front of her and to two others at the side. 'You must all be hungry after your trek,' she said. 'I have prepared maize meal and beans and chicken for us. Let us eat first and then I will explain everything to you.'

Once they had eaten, they settled on mats in front of Aiyasha, just like the Bundu Bunch used to do at her ABC classes.

Aiyasha began her story. 'First, let me tell you why it is that you find me here. This is where my father brought me from Bundami after my mother died when I was two years old. My father was a pastor. In Bundami he struggled to unite the community in support of those who could not afford to make contributions to the church celebrations and upkeep. In this matter, he clashed with Meyego, who persuaded the church to find another pastor. My father came here, to this remote part of the Mountain Kingdom, where everyone worked together to survive in these very harsh conditions. When, like my father, I needed to leave my past behind, I came here.

'When I was here with my father, I went to a mission school two valleys beyond this one. We didn't have a pony. It took three hours to walk to the school, but if I ran it took me just two hours. Running meant I could leave one hour later and get home one hour sooner. Two extra hours in the day to help my father keep house and tend the goats and chickens. Running up and down these hills became second nature to me. And I loved the freedom I felt as I ran. When I was fifteen, my father died. We buried him outside the stone church he had built and I was sent back to Bundami. Meyego sent me to the orphan hut and told me I must take charge of seven younger children who had just been orphaned. You were those orphans and we became a new family.'

Aiyasha paused for a moment, as she revelled in the memory of those times with her father and of running free in these mountains.

She then continued. 'Now, let me tell you why I needed to leave my past and to come here. My plan was to unite the people of Initawse. I wanted people to realise it was in the best interest of everyone to have equal opportunities, to contribute their talents to the benefit of the community as a whole. I had begun to implement my plan by getting the privileged to experience inequality in a way they had never experienced before. A way that was a disadvantage to themselves.

'And this was working. The privileged were protesting. Their placards indicated they were protesting against me and my policies. But, in reality, they were protesting at having to face inequalities that worked against them. If I could get out of the way, then it would become clearer to them that their protest was not about me, but about the unfairness of inequality and that inequity needs to be ended, whoever is advantaged or disadvantaged by it.

'At the same time, I had been told I was suffering from lung cancer and had just five years to live. I did not want my illness to become a distraction. I met with the Chief Headman and got an undertaking from him that my education policies would not be changed. In return, I would disappear from the scene and not expose his error in making my appointment. He agreed and he has kept his promise.

'I got my ministerial driver to take me to Bundami to meet with Meyego at the orphan hut. The Chief Headman had also agreed to my other condition, that headmen would be elected by communities in the future, instead of being appointed. He told me the most important headman holding out against this reform was Meyego, and I needed to persuade him to change his mind.

'As we all know, Meyego was a vain man. He liked to have things that made him feel special and important. I told him I was donating my gold medals to Bundami on the condition that free and fair elections were held. The first medal would be for him as a reward for agreeing to the elections. The second gold medal would be worn as a badge of authority by the new headman and all future elected headmen of Bundami. I gave him the first medal then and there, and kept the other one on account. He agreed.

'Now, all I had to do was to go somewhere I could hide and stay safe and observe the developments in Initawse. So I came here. To ensure nobody knew where I was, I had to get here without anyone seeing me. My problem was that my face was known by everyone in the country and I had to travel two hundred miles across it and across the border into the Mountain Kingdom without being recognised.

'I ran at night, along the tops of the hills where nobody lived. As I ran, I felt joyful and optimistic that my plan might actually work.

'And, as you know, it did.'

'Then Elah,' wrote Sipho, 'Aiyasha smiled. She nodded her head and looking at us she said slowly *The Bundu Bunch.*'

Aiyasha paused while she looked directly at each of us. Then she said 'It was due to you that I developed and implemented my plan. The way you all responded to my ABC classes in the forest gave me the motivation for and belief in my education policy. Thank you, I am very grateful to you all. And I am so proud of all you have achieved.'

Aiyasha paused again before saying, 'Please tell Elah that I am equally grateful to her. It was Elah's clear thinking that righted my way when I wavered. She believed in me, understood me and supported me. By challenging me and my decisions, she cemented my resolve. I am proud to learn she is doing so well as a teacher where her empathy and understanding will bring success through her students. There is no more important talent you can have than that.'

* * *

When I read this, tears came into my eyes. I now knew I no longer had to compare myself against the talents and achievements of The Bundu Bunch. We had all played an equal part in rewarding Aiyasha for the love and care she had given us in our early orphan years. And she was equally proud of all of us.

* * *

I met Audrey and Olivia at Leeds Bradford airport when they returned from Initawse. Without saying anything, we hugged each other tight and remained like that for a long while. When our emotions allowed us to separate, we held hands and walked out of the airport. We still hadn't said anything.

Later Olivia told me that, before they started back down the mountain, Aiyasha said, 'Please give this second gold medal to Samu and congratulate him on being elected as the new Headman of the Bundami community. Tell him I promised his father I would donate it to be worn by all elected leaders of Bundami as a mark of their commitment to equal opportunity for all.'

Audrey added, 'It was Monica who took the medal. She told Aiyasha that she would give it to Samu, with her message. Monica also said that one of them would visit every week. Aiyasha was very pleased to hear that and waved us all goodbye with a happy smile.'

* * *

It was two years later when I joined Audrey, Olivia and the Bundu Bunch at the ceremony where we buried Aiyasha in a grave next to her father, as she had wished. With her we buried her briefcase. Aiyasha was just fifty years old.

Chapter 11

Mkhulu's tales of long-ago times

There was a very old man in Bundami. Nobody knew just how old he was. When asked, all he would say was, 'Boniface was my uncle. I learnt how to tell stories from him.' Everybody called the old man Mkhulu.

I don't remember Boniface's storytelling. I was only just born then. But the Bundu Bunch orphans told me about the Boniface stories and how they set their imaginations alight.

Although every household now had their own smartphones, Bundami was one of the first communities in Initawse to ban the use of smartphones by children to communicate between themselves. Instead, children gathered together after school to interact through games, joint projects and communal downtime. The children particularly loved to gather at the preschool yard on a Saturday evening, just as it was getting dark. They gathered there to listen to Mkhulu, who sat in front of a fire and told them stories about long-ago times.

Many of these stories were about a good witch called Themba, a name that means 'hope'. This witch did not have a broomstick. But she had legs like wings that could carry her far and wide. She could be seen on nights of the full moon running across the tops of the mountains on her way to help families in trouble.

Mkhulu would start his stories about witch Themba by saying how things were very different in those long-ago-times.

'In those long-ago times, there were many households that needed Themba's help. In those days, lots of things were different in Bundami. The community was divided between the privileged and the poor. Most families were poor. The maize did not grow very well and the poor often starved, while the privileged got fat. There was a virus disease for which there was no vaccine. The mums and dads of poor families died from the disease, while the privileged bought medicines to keep themselves alive. The most extraordinary thing about those long-ago times was that privileged families were allowed to gain unfair advantage for their children, by paying to send them to the best schools with the best teachers and the best facilities. This perpetuated the divide between the privileged and the poor.'

According to Mkhulu, in those times lots of families needed help from Themba. And this help had to be provided in secret, so that the privileged did not get to hear about it and put a stop to it. Mkhulu told many exciting stories of how Themba managed to help poor families and how they managed to keep this a secret from the privileged few.

I'm not sure what all the children thought about these stories. But I like to think they helped them to appreciate their modern ways, where everyone had an equal opportunity to develop to their full potential. And, maybe, they helped some to become determined never to return to the ways of Mkhulu's long-ago days.

What I do know, though, is that many of the children would go outside when there was a full moon to look out for Witch Themba running across the tops of the mountains. And, some of them even told me they had seen her.

I smiled to myself as I thought about how Aiyasha, who had been seen as an evil witch by her Bundami community, had become the benevolent witch of national folklore. A magical legacy of many real, yet magical, lives of "dumb" orphans.

Epilogue

Eight years after Aiyasha's death, Samu, now elected President of Initawse, celebrated his fiftieth birthday. In his message to the nation, he reflected on Aiyahsa's pioneering work and how her resourcefulness and bravery had turned around the fortunes of his people. He announced that, to honour Aiyasha's life and work, the name of the country would be turned around and changed from Initawse to Eswatini.

Acknowledgements

I am grateful for the comments from readers of early drafts, including Bridget Gevaux and Jim Sweet. Jim in particular made useful observations, put me straight on some cultural matters and encouraged me to consider publication. I also owe a debt to Elizabeth Sparg who fitted the illustrations work between other prior commitments and who designed and created the cover.

About the author

Allan Low has worked with rural communities in Eastern and Southern Africa over a span of forty five years. He first worked with families on improving their agricultural production. He wrote a book on how farm-households in the region respond to new farming technology. Eleven years ago Allan set up the charity SHAMBA with his late wife, Anne. SHAMBA works with communities to enable their most disadvantaged children from AIDS affected households gain access to high quality early childhood care and education through their 'Bright Future' preschools. Allan now lives in Wetherby, UK and continues to visit the charity and manage its work.

To see more about Allan's motivation for writing this children's book visit his author website:

www.alow.magix.net/allanlow